"Have you had much experience at being a fiancée?" Kahrun's lips twitched in amusement.

Sara shook her head. "No, neither pretend or real. It wouldn't work, you know, but thanks for the thought."

"It'll have to work. I see no other way out of this without complications on either side."

"Just a fiancée, right? Indefinite marriage date. Still in the getting-to-know-each-other stage?" she clarified.

"Show only," Kahrun confirmed. Any elation he felt he kept hidden. Maybe they could brush through after all. They'd have to pretend only until the deal was finalized in a few weeks, a month at the most....

Barbara McMahon's latest novel begins a brand-new miniseries from Harlequin Romance®

Welcome to

High Society Brides

Rich or royal...it's the wedding of the year!

We're inviting you to the most thrilling and exclusive weddings

Meet women who have always wanted the perfect wedding...but never dreamed that they might be walking up the aisle with a millionaire, an aristocrat, or even a prince!

But whether they were born into it, are faking it, or are just plain lucky—these women are about to be whisked off around the world to the playground of princes and playboys!

Are their dreams about to come true? If so, they might just find that they are truly fit for a prince....

Look out for more HIGH SOCIETY BRIDES, coming soon in Harlequin Romance®.

In March, bestselling author Rebecca Winters brings you

Bride Fit for a Prince (#3739)

THE SHEIKH'S PROPOSAL
Barbara McMahon

High Society Brides

TORONTO • NEW YORK • LONDON
AMSTERDAM • PARIS • SYDNEY • HAMBURG
STOCKHOLM • ATHENS • TOKYO • MILAN • MADRID
PRAGUE • WARSAW • BUDAPEST • AUCKLAND

To my dear friend Tanaz Doroudchi.
Knowing you enriches my life!

ISBN 0-373-03734-1

THE SHEIKH'S PROPOSAL

First North American Publication 2003.

CHAPTER ONE

HER father was going to kill her, she thought, barely suppressing a groan. Sara Kinsale looked around the dusty cell and grimaced. She'd been here two days. Two days when she should have been at the hotel in Staboul. Two days stuck in some backwater jail in the very country in which her father was trying to nail the biggest deal of all time. When he needed everything perfect to convince the powers that be that his company could broker the most favorable deal for the newly-up-for-grabs oil leases.

She jumped up from the narrow cot and began to pace the tiny cell. She'd alternated between contemplating her parents' reaction with impatient pacing all the while trying to come up with a solution to her dilemma that might allow her to keep this from them and the world press.

If her father didn't kill her, her mother would guilt her to death with her soft sighs and her telling looks. She'd ask her father a million times, "Where did we go wrong?"

Sara blew her bangs off her forehead and leaned against the hard cinder block wall. She knew the drill. Her parents hadn't gone wrong, she had. But not intentionally. Things just seemed to go awry when she was involved.

First, she hadn't settled on any one career. Not like

her sister the attorney. Or her brother the nuclear physicist. Or even her mother, the perfect hostess, charity coordinator and helpmate to an international businessman.

She'd tried to find a niche that she could call her own. Acting hadn't worked out, to the great relief of her parents. Nor had nursing. She got queasy at the sight of blood. Being a child-care worker had been lots of fun, she loved playing with the kids. But her lack of discipline with the children had gotten her fired from both jobs she'd found.

The latest job might have bordered on acceptable—photojournalism was a respected profession. If she proved herself, maybe her family would begin to see her as a contributing member of society and not a flake who couldn't settle on anything.

Only now she'd blown that, as well. The editor of the U.S. tabloid newspaper that had hired her had been thrilled when she had told him about her upcoming visit to Kamtansin, one of the newly emerging Arabian countries on the Mediterranean Sea. The plum assignment of filming the royal enclave and getting photos of some of the royal family of the small Arabian country had been hers for the asking.

Interviewing some of the leading members of Kamtansin society had seemed a piece of cake in Los Angeles. Especially since several were in deep negotiations with her father over the oil leases. She'd meet them, bowl them over with her charm and get those photographs.

The reality proved one hundred percent opposite.

She'd been refused the interviews and refused photo opportunities.

The worst, however, was being apprehended trying to film the summer retreat of one of the leading families, despite being warned not to approach them. Now she languished in some horrible jail that didn't even have basic facilities.

Worse, she'd been accused of being a spy!

She'd not been allowed to contact the U.S. embassy. Nor call her father. She had not been permitted to seek an attorney. She had not been able to do anything but fret about the predicament she was in!

Her parents would be frantic. She'd stayed one night in the hotel with them when she first arrived. Then boldly plunged into her trip to get something on film after the string of refusals through normal channels. Even though she couldn't get close to the summer enclave she'd targeted, the telephoto lens would allow her to capture the finest details.

But she'd scarcely shot two views before being captured.

Her parents' worry couldn't compare with her own. The laws of this country were completely unknown to her. Would she be granted a trial, or end up remaining in this hot, dusty cell forever—with no one in her family ever knowing what happened to her?

The door opened. At least she had more privacy than she might have expected. The door to the small cinder block cell was solid wood, with only a small square about midway that permitted food to pass through twice a day, and allowed the jailors to check on her from time to time. Like she was going to escape? The only window in the room was equally small, and set too high in the wall for her to even reach.

The tall man dressed in the traditional Arab robes motioned with his head. He didn't speak English and she didn't understand a word of Arabic.

Sara brushed down her khaki trousers and shook her shirt a little. After two days and two nights with no washing, the sharp creases and crisp look had long since faded. She felt rumpled, dirty and tired. And more than a bit scared.

"I want to call the U.S. embassy," she said. She wasn't sure the man understood English, but she'd go down trying!

He remained silent, pointing down the hall.

She walked toward the door. Once within reach, he clasped her arm in a firm grip then marched her down the long corridor to the wide stairs at the end. Again she wondered what they thought she was going to do—flee from the building and face endless miles of burning desert sand and scorching heat with no vehicle to carry her back to safety? Her hired car was probably still hidden in the hill behind the summer villa. And she had no idea where that was in relation to where she was now.

They climbed two flights. He knocked on a door and upon hearing the reply from within, opened it, pushing Sara in before releasing her.

Sara quickly glanced around. It was an austere office with minimal furniture, no coverings on the windows. A man stood by one of the tall windows, gazing out over the desert landscape. She wasn't sure exactly where this jail was in relation to the capital city, but it wasn't far from the ruling family's retreat—the summer home she had tried to capture on film in order to have something for her newspaper's readers. Something to prove to her boss she was capable of the assignment.

Slowly he turned and looked at her.

Sara felt a warm tendril of awareness curl within when his eyes met hers. He easily stood taller than six feet. His hair was black, gleaming in the sunshine beaming in through the tall window. His eyes were dark, fathomless, with an uncompromising glint in them as he studied her. His cheekbones were high with taut tanned skin covering them. Power seemed to radiate from him, enhanced by the exquisitely tailored suit, the wide shoulders, the decidedly masculine stance. She felt the power through his study of her.

Suddenly aware of her own bedraggled appearance, she wished she could have brushed her hair or washed her face. Done something!

Then the absurdity of the situation hit her. She wanted to get out of this jail, not make some kind of good impression on a stranger. One, moreover, who apparently had some control over her incarceration, else why was she here?

"I wish to call the U.S. embassy," she repeated for at least the hundredth time.

He said something in Arabic and the man behind Sara bowed and left, closing the door.

"Sit," he said in English.

She blinked and looked around, spotting a chair against the wall beside the door. She'd have to pass by the desk to reach it. There was a phone on the desk, a few folders—one opened. Was that on her?

"I'm an American citizen. I wish to call the U.S. embassy. This has been a mistake that can be easily cleared up."

"Sit." It was clearly an order.

Moving quickly, Sara sat gingerly on the edge of the chair. Gorgeous or not, his manners needed work.

He stepped behind the desk and fingered a sheet of paper in the opened file. "You were arrested attempting to photograph a private dwelling—one which had posted signs warning trespassers away. You were trying to photograph members of the ruling family without permission. You carried no passport or other identification." He looked at her. "How did you get into this country and for what purpose?"

Sara swallowed. She needed to keep her father out of this imbroglio if possible. She could just imagine the result of his business negotiations if the world's press caught wind of the situation. Yet she couldn't stay here forever. She couldn't!

"My passport and other identification are in my room." She'd traveled light when heading out on assignment. A blessing, or a curse this time?

"And that would be where?"

Dare she tell him? Would he be discreet, believing she meant no harm? Releasing her to return to the capital city? His dark eyes held her gaze as if by merely looking at her he could determine if she spoke the truth or not.

"At the Presentation Hotel in Staboul."

He tilted his head slightly. "First-class accommodations," he said, flicking a glance over her disheveled clothing.

She cleared her throat and tried to smile brightly. "I have a room there, with my family."

"And that family would be?"

Who was this man? His suit was the finest Italian cut. His shirt a pristine white contrasting dramatically with his dark maroon tie. His hair was cut short, and he carried himself with an arrogant air. He looked sophisticated and urbane. And from the way the other man had bowed out of the room, the stranger was apparently someone of rank in this country. How susceptible would he be to keeping quiet about her identity?

"If you'd just let me make a call—"

He shook his head. "First, tell me who you are and why you were photographing the summer residence?"

"I'm Sara K— Sara Kay. I'm a newspaper photographer on assignment. I was just trying to get some photos to show Americans what the sheikh's home looked like. Your ruling family is very secretive—especially since the death of one of the sheikhs six months ago. We're curious, that's all. There's nothing sinister about it."

"Then why not request permission to make the photographs through normal channels?"

"I tried, no go."

"And did you not think there might be a reason for that?" His voice was hard, with an edge that set Sara's back up.

"Like what?"

"Privacy, perhaps?" he said softly.

"In America, once a family is in the public eye, their privacy is gone. The general public wants to know all about them."

"You are not in America."

Sara nodded, eyeing the phone. She couldn't snatch it up and dial her parents. She hadn't a clue how to reach the hotel. And she had a feeling this man would easily stop her if she made any attempt.

"Look, if you just let me make one call, I can get this all cleared up. Or you could let me go. The other guys took my camera. I don't have the film, so no harm done. I promise not to photograph anything ever again if you want. Can I just go?" Preferably with her expensive camera, but at this point, Sara would be grateful just to be allowed to leave.

He closed the folder with finality. Her heart sank. He wasn't going to let her waltz out of here. She'd have to use her family's name, call on the influence of her father. She bit her lip. There had to be another way. Her father would kill her!

"Your actions have put into motion a chain of events that could have serious repercussions," he said slowly.

"From trying to take a few pictures?"

"You are an American. My country is in the midst of delicate negotiations with American business entities over oil reserves recently discovered here in Kamtansin. There are factions in the country who do not wish to work closely with the Americans. The ministers are watching to make sure our country has the best representation. There are those factions who want the country to move into a new direction. The money the leases would bring in would go a long way to improving the standard of living for all our citizens. Your actions could jeopardize the entire negotiations.''

Sara swallowed. ''You could just let me go,'' she almost whispered. ''I wouldn't tell a soul.''

''Too many people already know you are here and what you did. The charge is espionage. We do not take kindly to people flaunting our laws. You requested permission to film and were denied. How would you describe your actions?''

''I wasn't spying!''

He continued as if she hadn't interrupted. ''The old guard would love nothing more than to prove to the world that we will not tolerate a flaunting of our laws and customs. They wish to make an example of you. It would add weight to our side of the negotiations, as well.''

Oh, great. This was the single biggest screwup she'd ever committed—and could ruin her father's business deal! She could just hear her mother!

''On the other hand, if negotiations are to continue for the oil leases, we dare not risk alienating the Americans by holding one of their citizens to make an example of her. If you truly work for a newspaper, I imagine the press coverage would be rampant.''

She watched him closely. Please decide on the don't-alienate-the-American side, she prayed, realizing the full impact of the situation. She felt a little sick with that realization. She'd only been trying to get pictures for the paper—nothing sinister. She had never envisioned causing an international incident. And she certainly didn't want to jeopardize her father's negotiations.

The door opened behind her. She turned to see the man who had brought her to the room. He spoke rapidly in Arabic. The man behind the desk nodded.

"Go, now," he said in English, turning back to the window deep in thought.

"Wait," Sara said, pulling against the grasp the other man took on her arm. "Please, let me call the hotel, my father can vouch for me. He's Samuel Kinsale. He knows the sheikh!"

Kharun froze at the words. The woman's father was Samuel Kinsale? The man with whom he had been working with for weeks in negotiating oil leases? He spun around and looked at her again.

Her bedraggled appearance didn't suggest the daughter of one of the world's most powerful men, but two days in a local jail could explain that. The prison facilities in his country were not known for their lavish appointments.

Her honey-blond hair needed brushing, but it still looked soft as a woman's hair should. Her expressive gray eyes flashed and sparkled as every emotion showed in her face. Her clothes, if clean and pressed, would have been easily recognized as top quality. He should have noticed that first thing.

But what was that story she gave about being a photographer? Was that a cover? Was she in truth acting as a spy, just like Hamin, Garh and their cohorts claimed?

Trying to find a weakness in their side her father could use to hammer out a better deal?

Or was she just foolishly blundering in where she had no business being?

"And what is the daughter of an American oil magnate doing spying on my family?"

"Your family?"

"I'm Kharun bak Samin. That home you were trying to photograph belongs to my family."

"Oh, sheesh, I'm in deep trouble now!" she said with a groan. At least she was consistent, the older she got, the bigger the mistakes she made.

"You have just made the situation a hundred times worse." He switched to his native tongue and told Jabil to return the woman to her cell. Watching as she protested, he let no expression show on his face. He'd become good at hiding his thoughts during negotiations. Never let the other person know his feelings, had been his motto. It stood him in good stead now.

As soon as they'd left, he turned back to the window. But he didn't see the oasis to the left with the soaring date palms, the green grass that flourished in the midst of the sandy desert, or the drab houses of those who eked out an existence on the edge of the dunes. Nor did he see the endless desert beyond that stretched out to Morocco, wild and free and beckoning.

He saw instead the council chamber he'd left that morning. His uncle's handpicked ministers fighting against the men his father had recommended for the council. New regime against the old. Antiquated ways clashing against the hope of moving his country firmly into the twenty-first century.

And smack in the middle came the daughter of the man he was negotiating for oil leases that would enable the government to make the reforms his father had so longed for.

He had involved himself in the situation before he knew all the facts. Now others knew of his involvement. So the final decision would be his. What to do with Sara Kinsale?

Both sides would be closely watching. His father had served on the council for years, the old faction knew him. Now they watched to see he didn't sell out the country. The newer ministers were still wary about moving forward too quickly, wondering if he had the capability to represent their country in the treaty negotiations. They had trusted his father, and transferred that trust to him. But still, they watched.

Their country was such a dichotomy—rich and modern in the cities, poor and underdeveloped in the desert areas. With the influx of funds the oil leases would provide, much more could be done for the outlying areas—bringing all citizens into the twenty-first century.

Whatever he decided, it must be handled discreetly and with great diplomacy. His years in business had taught him all he needed. Now it was time to implement a strategy to get them out of this sticky situation.

He turned and reached for the phone.

Sara lay on her cot, wishing it had a modicum of comfort. Lumpy and narrow, it was obviously not geared for the Ritz. She'd played her trump card—given her father's position—and it hadn't helped. Maybe the oil leases weren't as important as she thought. Or maybe the sheikh felt he held the trump card with her in jail. Maybe he'd use that to force her father into giving concessions.

She groaned, wishing she'd never started this chain of events!

For the first time since her arrest she considered the possibility of staying in jail for a long time. She shivered, not liking the prospect at all.

She closed her eyes—seeing Kharun bak Samin. The top businessman dealing with her father, nephew of the chosen leader of this beautiful Arabian country. The son of the sheikh who had recently died, and who had played an important role as adviser to the ruler. Things could not possibly be worse. What would her father say?

Restless with her thoughts, she sprang up again and began to pace the small space. If her lapse of good sense resulted in negotiations breaking down, it could mean her father losing the deal—another company getting the oil rights. A major contract going south because of her impetuousness.

What would the sheikh decide?

She tried to blank out the memory of that fluttering of interest in the man—personal interest. Was the desert heat getting to her? He had been part of her assignment—photograph the elusive Kharun bak Samin. Let the women of America get a good look at one of the world's most eligible bachelors—heir to the fortune built by his father and enhanced by his own efforts. Dynamic businessman of this important country on the Mediterranean Sea, and handsome as a movie star.

She'd thought it would be a snap, that she'd be able to sell the story and pictures and make a name for herself with the newspaper. She had wanted the credentials of a job well done to help her move to a more established newspaper. One that delivered news and commentaries, not sensationalism.

Trying to ignore the twinge she felt every time she thought about the tabloid aspect of her job, she focused on the fact it was a step toward more serious photojournalism.

But she couldn't help remembering how she herself cringed when seeing the flashy headlines splashed across the different tabloids at the grocery store checkout stands.

Her impetuosity had once again gotten her in trouble. But this time, her father could also suffer. She'd paid little attention to his plans recently, more concerned with learning how to operate the fancy camera she'd bought for the trip, and trying her hand at reporting news.

The two articles she written that had been accepted had been changed beyond recognition by the time they hit the stands. She tried for the exploitive tone of the paper, but it proved impossible.

She had really wanted to do this story—always hoping for the best—a human interest kind of story, nothing sensational.

Sara couldn't bear the thought of being the one to bring disgrace on her father. All she'd ever wanted was to make him proud of her. Now this. She should have kept her mouth shut! She should never have told the sheikh who she was. Sara Kay was an unknown, no one would rally around to rescue her.

But the daughter of Samuel Kinsale? Her father would spare no expense to find her. And if he didn't like the way she'd been treated, he'd stop the negotiations in a heartbeat.

Pacing back and forth, she wished she could go back in time three days. Wished she could turn back the clock. Would she have done anything differently?

Not get caught, for one thing. But the only way she could have avoided that, if she had the last three days to do over, was to not attempt the photo shoot. She'd gambled her career on that. Gambled and lost.

The afternoon hours dragged. Another day gone and she was no nearer to getting back to her family—or even letting them know she was all right.

Kharun seethed with impatience and frustration. His calls had given him the information he needed—Sara Kinsale was indeed the daughter of the man he was dealing with. The youngest child of a very worried man who was discreetly trying to locate his missing daughter.

Samuel Kinsale, too, was aware of the delicacy of the negotiations. And for the time being, didn't seem interested in upsetting the balance. But that would change if he didn't locate his daughter soon.

What would he do when he found out his daughter was in jail being held on charges of espionage?

Kharun's trusted adviser, Piers, suggested secreting her away, hiding her until after the oil leases were signed. But Kharun didn't see that as a viable option. Keeping her whereabouts hidden from her parents for weeks or months would be needlessly cruel.

Garh Sonharh, leader of the old guard, had been vocal in pushing for full prosecution. Kharun had not spoken to him directly—holding off as long as possible as he mulled the situation over. But he'd heard of Garh's wishes from Piers. Once he spoke directly with his uncle's strongest minister, he would be committed.

Kharun's call to his sister hadn't helped. She'd sympathized, discussed the situation, then offered a bizarre idea for scraping through unscathed. Bizarre nothing—it was plain stupid from start to finish.

Damn! He rose from behind the desk and paced the narrow room, wishing he could get on his horse and ride out into the desert until the entire situation made some kind of sense. The freedom he enjoyed on the back of Satin Magic brought a soothing almost mystic release to tension and turmoil.

But his horse was at his summer villa by the sea, and he was here, fifty miles inland.

Beside, he didn't think Garh would take kindly to being ignored while Kharun went horseback riding.

He smiled cynically. It didn't matter what he did, Garh didn't approve.

Nor did his aunt. If she had her way, his tenure as negotiator would be short. But he had the international business experience to know what to bargain for and to stand for his principles. His uncle trusted him, as had his father.

The bottom line—Kharun had the final recommendation regarding the oil leases. His uncle, the ruler of their country, had utmost faith in him. He had better do something soon before it all blew up in his face.

For the first time, he gave his sister's suggestion serious thought. It was a dumb way to muddle through a crisis, but might be the only way to save face all around. And it would make it very difficult for Garh to carry out his threat for an espionage charge.

He summoned Sara Kinsale.

She entered the room with her head held high. Jabil released her and bowed out, closing the door.

"I want to call the American embassy," she said firmly.

Kharun's lips almost twitched in amusement. She had her own strength, he noted, beginning to notice other things about her. She was taller than the average height of most of the women in his country, and that honey-blond hair shone like a beacon. She'd stand out in a crowd. She carried herself proudly. The curves the khakis displayed were womanly and alluring.

He jerked his gaze back to her blazing eyes. Silvery when she was angry, a light gray when not. If she went for the bizarre suggestion, he wondered if he'd be able to gauge her moods by the color of her eyes alone?

"I have confirmed your identity. Your father is escalating his search for you. Pretty soon it will be impossible to keep the circumstances private. Not that you will mind, will you? Once a public figure, privacy is lost, correct?"

She narrowed her eyes as she gazed at him, obviously not liking her own words thrown back.

"I apologize for infringing on your family's privacy. Next time I'll make sure I have permission for a photo shoot."

"Next time?"

She shrugged, still standing proudly before him.

All her makeup had long since worn off. Her cheeks had a natural color to them, and her lips looked full and sweet.

Kharun frowned and looked away from the tempting lips. He needed to make sure they both understood the proposal—and not get confused with some fantasies about the delectable femininity before him.

"I spoke briefly about the situation and the possible repercussions earlier," he began.

She nodded. "I didn't mean to cause problems."

"There may be a way out of this quagmire with a bit of acting on both our parts. Are you willing to hear my proposal?"

She nodded. Her shoulders relaxed a bit. Was she relieved to let him find a way out of the mess? Thus far she'd come up with nothing.

"I suggest we pretend to the world that we have known each other for some time. That your trip to visit your family is merely a cover to see me. That we became secretly engaged and you were planning on surprising me with photos of my family's home as an engagement present."

She stared at him, not moving. Had she heard what he said?

"Are you totally crazy?" she asked at last, almost exploding the words. "Engaged? As in get married to each other one day? No one in their right mind would believe such a thing! Where did you ever come up with such a ridiculous idea? I can't believe that's the best you can come up with. Aren't you supposed to be some hotshot businessman? This is your proposal? I can counter it in a heartbeat—just let me go. I won't say a word. Make up something—like you imposed a heavy fine. I can't believe you can't think of a rational reason to release me without repercussions!"

He let her rant and rave for a couple of minutes, fascinated by her passion. Her eyes blazed, her breasts rose and fell as she drew in deep breaths. Her cheeks were flushed with color. Would she look as enticing in bed?

Where had that thought come from? He had no intention of finding out. He was trying to get through this without either side losing.

He held up a hand for silence. She closed her mouth and glared at him. He almost smiled at the picture she presented. However, now was not a time to get sidetracked.

"On the surface, I agree it does seem strange."

Hadn't he ranted and raved at his sister only a couple of hours ago protesting the very idea? "But there is a hint of merit in the idea. Hear me out. If we are allied, if we have a personal reason for your taking pictures of forbidden areas, we can scrape through both the ministers's anger and the embarrassment you'd cause your father if his daughter was publicly prosecuted and condemned. An engagement would only be temporary—until the lease negotiations are finalized. At that point, you can return home and we'll make a joint statement that there were too many differences to overcome.''

She blinked and continued to study him. "It'd never work," she said at last. "No one would ever believe you'd fall for me.''

That caught him by surprise. "Why not? You're pretty and adventuresome—traits which would appeal to any man. We could have met in any number of cities we've both visited.''

"Puh-lease. You're the nephew of the ruler of this country. Your own father was an important member of the council before his death. I'm the flaky younger daughter of an oil dealer. If it was my sister, Margaret, I could see it, maybe. She's sophisticated, successful and never puts a step out of place. You don't even want to *suggest* such a proposal with me.''

For a second he wanted to agree with her. But it wasn't for real. Just a mock engagement to appease the ministers and keep scandal from rocking a still precariously run country. And, of course, to ensure the negotiations concerning their newly discovered oil reserves could continue with no awkwardness.

"It would take very little on your part—pretend to be my fiancée, attend a few social events, stay at my place temporarily. You do have some acting skills, surely.''

She shook her head. "Been there, done that. Didn't take.''

"What?''

"I tried acting. I'm no good at it. That I don't fully

embrace the character, was the kindest criticism I received. The rest pretty much said I was a total flop."

"Have you had experience at being a fiancée?"

She shook her head. "Nope, neither pretend nor real. It wouldn't work, you know, but thanks for the thought. Can't you just let me go?"

"It will have to work, I see no other way out of this without complications on one side or the other. The next best suggestion was to secret you away to another facility and play ignorant while your parents worry and search fruitlessly for you. Is that a better choice? Or are you ready for the repercussions that could arise out of being tried for espionage?"

He saw he'd hit home with his first comment. She didn't wish to worry her parents any more than he did. She knew what a trial would do to her father's negotiations. Would she agree to this ludicrous scheme now that he'd played that card? One way or another it was up to him to ensure the negotiations continued with a favorable result. Would she make it easier or harder?

"Just a fiancée, right? Indefinite marriage date. Still in the getting-to-know-each-other stage?" she clarified.

"Show only," he confirmed. Any elation he felt, he kept hidden. Maybe they could brush through, after all. They'd only have to pretend until the deal was finalized in a few weeks, a month at most.

"Okay, then, I guess I'll have to agree. Now can I make a call?"

Before Kharun could respond, the phone rang. He answered it, his eyes never leaving Sara. Could he trust her to fulfill her part? Trust that once she left the jail she wouldn't flee the country and to hell with the consequences?

Or would she hang around hoping to get those pictures that had her risking everything earlier this week?

"Garh, here, Kharun. I've heard some interesting rumors about an American spy you're holding at the jail," the familiar voice said when Kharun picked up the phone.

"You need a better source for rumors, Garh. No spies here. A misunderstanding about a present my fiancée wanted to give me."

The pause was minuscule. "Fiancée? I had no idea you were engaged to be married. Your uncle made no mention of this to me. When did this happen?"

"Some time ago. Out of respect for my father's recent passing and the grief in my family at his death, we elected to wait until a more suitable time to announce our betrothal. However, her zeal to capture the family home as a gift for me has changed our timing. We will let everyone in the family know immediately."

"Interesting, I didn't even know you knew Samuel Kinsale's daughter, much less had enough time for a courtship." Suspicion was evident in his tone.

Kharun remained silent. The less he told the old manipulator, the less he had to remember and deal with later.

But wasn't it interesting that Garh knew who Sara was. How had he found out? Kharun had only found out himself a couple of hours ago when Sara told him.

"And when is the wedding?" Garh asked silkily.

"We haven't set a date yet."

"Ah."

Kharun felt the hair on the back of his neck rise. He didn't trust Garh as far as he could throw him. What was the wily minister thinking?

"Perhaps you should consider setting the date immediately. It is one thing to excuse a flighty fiancée, yet engagements can be so easily broken, correct? It would be something else to forgive a dutiful wife."

Kharun heard the threat in his tone. And knew his sister's idea hadn't been foolproof. Was Garh calling his bluff?

"Perhaps you are correct. I will let you know the date. In the meantime, Sara and I will be returning to the capital this evening if you need to reach me again."

He hung up and stared at the phone. The man suspected a coverup. Of all the ministers, Garh pushed the hardest to hear other proposals for oil sales. Kharun couldn't give him any power to stall the current negotiations.

He looked at Sara harshly. "The plan has changed. We will be married immediately."

CHAPTER TWO

SARA gazed out the limousine window, amazed at how fast things had spun out of control. She longed to look at the man seated beside her, but didn't dare make eye contact, or give him any reason to suspect she was interested in him beyond his being the one responsible for rescuing her from jail.

The desert was cloaked in shadows, deep and mysterious as the sun set in the west. She'd caught a glimpse of an oasis when they'd left the enclave. And the heartbreaking sight of a little child scantily dressed, staring at the costly vehicle as they pulled away.

Somewhere out there was his luxurious family home. The contrast between what she'd glimpsed before being arrested and the tiny child at the side of the road was outrageous. Sara knew the same divisions of wealth existed all over the world, but they just seemed less dramatic.

The meagerness of amenities in the area had been apparent and appalling. Nothing like the bustling modernity of the capital city. How did the city people resolve living with their own abundance when they were surrounded by such destitution?

And who was this stranger next to her and how had she wound up agreeing to his scheme? Was there an alternative to his outrageous proposal? Her mind spun trying to find a solution that would suit them both.

As they sped toward the coast, she reviewed her options. Not many, if her word was to hold. Which it would. Her actions had precipitated the situation. If she could avoid a major scandal with no adverse repercussions to her father and his negotiations, it was important she do so.

Yet the thought of sneaking away in the dark and catching a ride home on the next available plane held a lot of appeal.

Should she just throw herself on her father's good nature and ask for help?

"It will take at least two hours to reach Staboul City," Kharun said from her left.

Sara glanced his way, startled to find his intense gaze focused on her. She felt a shiver of awareness. He seemed to fill the ample space of the limo, though he didn't crowd her to do so.

Upon entering the limousine, he'd closed the glass between them and the driver. They were cocooned in a world of two for the next couple of hours. She could smell his faint aftershave, spicy and masculine. She looked away, aware her heart rate had sped up a notch.

Just then the car hit a pothole, jerked, shuddered and quickly recovered, but not before throwing Sara against his hard chest. She scrambled to regain her seat, even more aware of the differences between them. She was tired, dirty and shaking off the fear of the last few days. He looked as immaculate as he must have done that morning.

He inclined his head slightly. "One of the benefits of the oil leases would mean funds to repair our roads. Perhaps you should fasten your seat belt."

"And help people in villages like the one we just left?" she asked, pulling the belt across her. She didn't want to wind up in his lap again.

"The treaty will allow us to do many things, including extending our education for all children, build new medical facilities, provide new jobs. Bring my country from a nomadic past into the technological future."

Swallowing hard, Sara tried to focus on the words and not the strange sensations that sparkled through her at his tone. She felt as if he'd touched her, when there were at least twelve inches of space between them. The very air seemed to crackle with tension.

She looked away, at the growing darkness. Two hours. It seemed like an interminable time to be cooped up with Sheikh Kharun bak Samin. Though not as long a time as it would be if she went through with his crazy scheme to get married.

"I suggest we use the time until we arrive to get to know each other. If we are to pull this off, I need to know more about you than you tried to take illicit photos in a restricted area and are the daughter of Samuel Kinsale."

"Will we be able to pull this off?" She had her doubts. Though she'd do nothing to harm her father's career, she was afraid her acting skills were far below what was needed to convince people she and this powerful man were in love. She wasn't even comfortable riding in a car with him. What would it be like to pretend devotion? To be touched by those strong hands, be caressed—

She shut down her mind. Taking a deep breath she tried for rational thought. Just because the man beside her was the sexiest male she'd ever met was no reason to lose coherent thought. She'd need all her wits about her if she was to come through unscathed.

"Shall I begin? Hello, I'm Kharun bak Samin." He held his hand out.

Reluctantly Sara placed hers in his, hoping for a quick, formal, means-nothing handshake. Did his comment mean he had a sense of humor? So far she'd seen no evidence of one.

His touch startled her. His hand was warm, firm, holding hers as if she was precious crystal. Tingling sensations danced on her nerve endings, causing her to catch her breath. She felt swept away to another level of existence, as if everything before was a prelude to this wondrous delight.

Snatching her hand free she tried to smile, but her facial muscles refused to cooperate. Her heart raced in her chest. Warmth infused her. She took a deep breath—a mistake since it filled her with his scent. She scrambled for coherence.

"How do you do? I'm Sara Kinsale, youngest child of Samuel and Roberta Kinsale." She could have added "classic misfit," but she had a feeling he suspected that already.

"Now where would we have met, Sara? Not here, this is your first visit to my country. Perhaps another locale to which your father has traveled frequently and I had an occasion to visit?''

"He's traveled all over Europe. I sometimes go with them. How about Paris?''

He appeared lost in thought for a moment, then nodded. ''That'll work. My mother is from France and I visit there often. I've been twice in the last couple of years. I assume you were there sometime during that time span?''

She nodded. ''I haven't lived with my folks since I left for college, but did travel with them a few months ago to Paris.'' She'd been between jobs and at loose ends. Shortly after she'd returned home, she'd landed the photojournalist position.

"So you graduated from college, which one?''

She named one of the famous Ivy League colleges, then frowned slightly. ''Only I didn't graduate. I never could settle on a major.''

"Photography and journalism not being an option?''

"Back when I was eighteen I had visions of following in my father's footsteps. I studied business administration for a while—but found it too heavily focused on math and economics. So then I thought about becoming an interpreter—my French is pretty good. That didn't take, either.''

"So the next course of study was?'' he prompted when she fell silent.

"Next I tried drama. I even had a role in one of the college productions. I didn't succeed beyond my wildest dreams. Actually I was a dismal actress. The reviews didn't even try to be kind. That's why I question how this plan of yours will work. How can I pretend to be your fiancée if my acting skills are nonexistent?''

"As my *wife,* you will be beyond questioning. As long as you can appear dutifully attentive when we are in public, there should be no problem.''

Her heart skipped a beat, resumed with a rapid pace.

"I can't marry you.''

"That was settled before we left the jail.''

"I know you said we had to marry, but think about it—it's crazy.''

He leaned toward her, his eyes hard as flint. "Listen well, Sara Kinsale. Your actions have jeopardized something important for my country. We are not the richest country on earth, with a standard of living above all others. Poverty and disease affect a lot of my people. I want to improve the lot and to do so we need an influx of cash. Your father is brokering an oil lease that will bring in that influx. It's the perfect solution and I will not have it destroyed by the flighty irresponsible actions of one woman. You will marry me, you will appear to be my dutiful wife in public and you will say nothing to anyone until that lease is signed, sealed and delivered. At that time, we can arrange a quiet annulment and you can return to your father's care.''

"Yes, sir!'' She tilted her chin. She was not intimidated by his words, but almost exhilarated. What was wrong with her? She should have been quaking in her shoes. Instead, her blood pounded in her veins, her senses were attuned to every nuance and she felt more alive than at any time in her life.

So he wanted marriage, did he? All right. She'd just show him what being married to her would entail!

"So where did you go to school? What's your favorite color and how come you're not already married?" she asked.

She kept surprising him. It had been a long time since someone had done that. For one moment when he challenged her he'd thought she'd quail under his glare. But that little chin came right up and she stood up for herself. If they'd been standing he had no doubt she would have stood toe-to-toe with him, tilting that stubborn chin and glaring at him with silver eyes.

Jasmine's idea had been ludicrous, but the longer he lived with it, the longer he was around Sara Kinsale, the more it grew on him. At the very least, it wouldn't be a boring marriage—however short.

He almost grinned at the surprise he envisioned on his aunt's face when she met his future bride. His uncle's wife liked to think she ruled the family. While always courteous and polite, Kharun was ruled by no one— especially his aunt who would have been happy living in the early days of the last century.

There would also be the possible added bonus of getting the country more firmly on his side. People always were drawn to the romantic, he thought cynically, wondering how they could put a positive spin on the situation. And counter the rumors Garh would be sure to spread.

"I attended Eton then Harvard, finishing with a graduate degree of business at Wharton in Pennsylvania," he said as he became aware she was waiting for his response.

"Oh." She sat back in her seat, eyeing him with a hint of respect—the first he'd seen in her gaze.

"My favorite color is green." Though silver might be moving up to the top spot. "And why I have not married is none of your business. Neither have you. Do you want to tell me why?"

She opened her mouth and he almost held his breath, wondering what she would come out with. When she snapped it shut and shook her head, he was disappointed.

"Did you know green is the color most likely to be a favorite of geniuses? Are you super smart?"

He questioned that, giving his plan to follow his sister's suggestion.

"Your favorite color?" he asked.

"Blue. Favorite ice cream is vanilla, boring, I know, but I love it. Favorite TV show is 'Star Trek,' any rendition that comes on. Favorite food is chocolate—made any way and every way it can be. I've been supporting myself since I left college. And I don't have any pets, though I always wished we could have a dog."

"Do you ride?"

She nodded. "Finest lessons to be had. Do you?"

"Yes. I have a couple of horses. Maybe we'll find we have something in common after all."

"We don't need anything in common. This is temporary. How long do you think it'll take to sign that deal? If you sign soon, we don't even have to get married."

"I have no way of knowing how long it'll take. If

everything goes smoothly, another few weeks. If we run into complications, it could take longer. We've already been in negotiations for four months.''

"Four months! Good grief, what's the holdup? I mean, don't you read the terms, agree or disagree, hammer them out and sign the darn thing?''

"It's a bit more complex than that. And having an American spy thrown into the mix doesn't help.''

"I'm not a spy,'' she said through gritted teeth.

"I would have thought a spy more adept at blending in, if nothing else.'' He glanced at her hair, still fascinated by it. His fingers itched to test its softness. He wondered if he twirled a curl around a finger if it would cling. "Your hair sets you apart from most of the people in the country. You would have done better to wear a hat or dye your hair.''

"Look, I'll make you a deal. You stop referring to me being a spy and I'll do my best to be an adoring fiancée.''

"Wife,'' he reminded her.

"Fine! Wife for as long as it takes to sign the blasted treaty.''

His cell phone rang. Kharun flipped it open and heard his sister's voice.

"So, what happened?'' Jasmine asked with no ceremony.

"My fiancée and I are on our way to my villa as we speak. There's been a slight change in the plans, however. Garh Sonharh found out about our visitor and began to question our relationship. We will be married immediately.''

Jasmine audibly gasped. "You're kidding. You're not going to actually *marry* the woman! Kharun, that's even more stupid than my original idea. An engagement is one thing—but *marriage?*"

"It is settled. We shall meet the rest of the family in the morning. Tonight would not be auspicious." He glanced at Sara, taking in the rumpled and stained clothing, the tiredness around her eyes, and the glare that met his gaze.

"I'm sorry I suggested the idea. You should listen to Piers, his idea made more sense," Jasmine said.

"We have settled the matter."

"You always were headstrong. Why not stick with the engagement and to hell with Garh? Or let her stay in jail. It's not worth risking your future."

"I can take care of my future. I'll call you in the morning, Jasmine."

"I thought you were taking me to the hotel," Sara said as soon as he'd disconnected.

"Perhaps I shall do that in the morning."

"In the morning? I want to go tonight!"

"Looking like you do? Wouldn't there be a question or two about where you've been and what you've been doing?" he asked silkily.

"I thought you were concerned about my parents worrying about me," she tried.

"My secretary has already phoned them to assure them you are well—and with me. What's more natural than lovers who haven't seen each other in months to wish to be reunited?"

"Lovers?" She almost squeaked the word.

He had not thought beyond the ceremony that would join them in marriage. He had not thought about the reality after their vows. Now he considered how difficult it might prove to be to ignore this woman when she was living in close proximity.

Her turn of mind already intrigued him. Her blond, silky hair drew his gaze time after time, and he found himself deliberately saying things to annoy her just to see the sparkle in her eyes.

She had passion in her. Would that passion carry over to bed? Would she be hot and wild and as captivating as Sheherazade?

For the right man, he had no doubt. Did she even suspect the direction of his thoughts? Was she having similar ones?

"We're not lovers!" she said.

"We could be."

"In your dreams."

"Time will tell."

"Hold on a minute. If you think getting married gives you the right to share my bed, we need to talk about this some more."

"It does give me the right. Whether I exercise that right or not remains to be seen."

"I have some say in this."

"Of course. The same vows give you the right to my bed."

"Oh."

She leaned back in her seat, her eyes wide, staring into space as if she'd just realized the full implication.

Kharun watched her in the dim illumination. She

looked lost and lonely and stunned with the thought. And imminently kissable. His gaze focused on her lips, damp from her tongue, faintly pink and full. What would she taste like? How would she respond if he pulled her into his arms and kissed her? Could he spark all that passion and have it focused on him?

"You stay out of my bed and I'll stay out of yours," she said at long last.

"Shall we continue our briefing?" He didn't agree with her suggestion. Had she noticed? Apparently not, she continued with a litany of likes and dislikes, of vignettes of family life and friends. He settled back to watch her, enjoying the play of emotions across her face. And he continued to fantasize about threading his hands in that silky hair and coaxing curls around his fingers.

It was long after dark when they arrived at his villa. A few miles outside of Staboul City, it hugged the sea. Seventeen acres of privacy, with a beach that he too rarely used. It had been a legacy to him from his father upon his death. He had offered his mother free access for her life and she sometimes resided with him for weeks at a time. Always leaving when the memories became too much and she needed a change of scenery.

For a moment he remembered how happy his parents had been in their marriage. Had his grandparents opposed the match? He'd never heard, but often wondered if they had approved of their son marrying a foreigner. Born in France, his mother had been raised in Morocco. She loved the desert, loved the culture and had adored his father.

His aunt had never fully accepted her sister-in-law. He had no doubts how she would react to his marriage to Sara. It was best done quickly. They could excuse the lack of celebration and ceremony to the untimely death of his father six months ago. His family was still in mourning.

"I smell the sea," Sara said.

"My house is on the beach. You can swim in the sea every day if you wish. Just make sure someone is around in case you get into trouble." During her recital of likes and dislikes, she'd revealed how much she loved the ocean. If nothing else, she should be content living here until they annulled their marriage.

He had made a quick call to his housekeeper when they'd been halfway home, requesting she make up a guest suite for his fiancée. She'd informed him of his mother's arrival. While he could have used another day or two before presenting Sara to his family, it wasn't all bad his mother was already in residence. He'd need all the allies he could get to pull this off. Jasmine would help. Now he'd have his mother on his side.

If only his aunt had taken a quick trip somewhere.

But life never ran smoothly. Look at the situation he was presently in.

"Wow, is that yours?" Sara gazed at the house, lit up from top to bottom as it awaited the return of its master.

"It is."

"It looks like a French villa, or something on the Spanish Riviera, not Arabian."

"My father built it for my mother. She is French. It

is a good thing your French is excellent. She'll love conversing in her native tongue. She learned Arabic, of course, but I know she misses her first language.''

"Maybe this isn't such a good idea. It's one thing to fool your ministers, but your mother?''

"Your parents, too.''

She looked at him. "I thought I could at least explain—''

He shook his head. "Unwise. One wrong word and the entire situation would blow up in our faces. I'd lose whatever steps I've gained and the lease negotiations would be crushed. Only you, me and Jasmine will know the truth.''

"Jasmine is your sister. Why can't I tell someone in my family?''

"No.''

The car slid to a stop before the large double doors. They were opened wide and a woman dressed in a uniform stood quietly to one side.

"Let's see if your acting skills have improved since college days,'' he said as the chauffeur opened the back door.

Sara climbed out, stiff and awkward.

Kharun spoke in Arabic when he asked if Sara's rooms were ready and Aminna responded in the affirmative. His housekeeper was efficient and discreet. And loyal—having been with his parents long before he inherited her services along with the villa.

"Your mother has already retired. I didn't know when you'd be home, so did not inform her of your guest,'' the older woman said.

"Well done, Aminna. Time enough in the morning."

He placed his hand in the small of Sara's back and urged her into the house. "I'll take you to your room," he said in English.

Sara had the impression of space as they hurried down the hallway in the direction he indicated. She'd barely glanced into the entrance, or the rooms beyond, though all were lighted. The ceilings were high. The terrazzo floors were cool beneath her feet and the walls were white, adding to the impression of space. The hall itself was wide, with doors opening off it here and there.

She couldn't take it all in at the pace he directed. Or with the tingling that had begun when his hand touched her back. She could barely walk! Fatigue had to be the cause. She'd not slept well the last two nights. For one foolish moment, she wanted to lean into that hand, rest against the strong shoulders that were so temptingly near.

Realizing how dumb the idea was, she stepped out of reach, but the tingling awareness lingered.

"If you just tell me which room is mine, I'll be fine."

He opened a door, and stepped aside for her to enter.

The bedroom was like a fairy-tale setting. French doors opened onto a veranda. The breeze from the sea billowed the gauzy curtains. The bed was huge, dominating one wall, with netting draped enticingly around it as if waiting to shelter a princess.

A small sitting area was carved out of one side. Beyond the bed a door stood open to a luxuriously appointed bathroom.

"A hot shower sounds wonderful," Sara said as her gaze skimmed across the furnishings, the cool floor beneath. What a dramatic change from the cell she'd inhabited for two nights.

"I'll make sure Aminna has something brought in for you to wear," Kharun said. "Please ring if you need anything." He stepped back into the hall, closing the door behind him.

Sara almost danced across the room. It was heavenly—and a light-year away from the tiny, dusty cell she'd been in that afternoon. She went to the French doors and peered outside. Flowers bloomed near the terrace, a path led away—to the sea?

She turned back. Time enough tomorrow to go exploring. Right now, she wanted that hot shower!

Stripping as she walked, she headed directly for the bathroom. She closed the door behind her and in seconds stood beneath the hot spray, relishing the feel of the water slipping over her body. Slowly she washed her hair, soaped her dusty skin.

As the warm water caressed her skin, her tired, traitorous mind imagined Kharun's hands caressing her body in a similar fashion, following the curves, touching her breasts, learning every inch of her. The heat that built within at the rampant thoughts matched the heat of the water.

A cold shower would be better, she thought, shampooing her hair for the second time. She wanted all trace of her recent experience expunged completely! She'd do better to spend her time thinking how to explain the situation to her father than imagining Kharun's hands roaming.

She wasn't usually given to flights of fancy. This was a platonic situation—forged from necessity, not need or want or desire. And she'd best remember that!

Finally giving in to the tiredness that threatened, she shut off the water. The towels were luxurious—in keeping with everything else she'd seen so far, thick and soft. She wrapped one around her, used another to swathe her hair.

She gazed around the bathroom. Except for her underwear lying on the tiles, she had nothing to wear. And she wouldn't wear them again until clean. Snatching them up, she quickly washed them in the sink and hung them over a towel rod to dry. They'd be ready by morning.

Opening the door, she stepped into the opulent bedroom. Maybe the housekeeper had placed a nightgown on the bed.

Sara stopped short. Kharun sat in one of the chairs in the sitting area, looking completely at home.

She gripped the towel. It was tucked firmly against her, nothing showed—indeed, it covered her almost to her knees. But she knew she had nothing beneath but damp skin, and that made her extremely vulnerable.

She glanced at the trail of dusty clothes and wanted to snatch them up, so he wouldn't notice. But of course he'd had ample time to notice. How long had he been in her room?

He raised an eyebrow, letting his gaze travel from her

wrapped hair, across damp shoulders, down the length of her.

Heat swept through her. Her heart began to pound heavily. She couldn't take her eyes off him.

"What are you doing in here?" she asked, going on the offensive.

He rose and started toward her. His hand held a gossamer nightgown. "I brought you something to sleep in."

She stared at the delicate material, knowing it was as light and sheer as the curtains that billowed in the breeze. She raised her gaze to meet his, surprised by the heat she saw. Her heart raced. Mesmerized by the look in his eyes, she couldn't move. Couldn't utter a word. The fantasy in the shower played out in her mind. She wanted to slam the door shut on the images, but couldn't.

He came so close she could feel the heat from his body, see the fine lines around his eyes, smell the male scent mingling with that from the sea air.

For a moment neither moved. Then slowly—oh, so slowly—he lowered his head, blocking out the room, blocking out everything except him.

When his lips touched hers, Sara gave a small sigh and closed her eyes. His lips were warm and firm, moving gently against hers.

She almost missed it when his arms encircled her, pulling her against his hard body. She was too busy wrapping her own arms around his neck; holding on as his kiss inflamed every cell. His embrace was hot and exciting, as he moved against her with sensuous pleasure. Her body felt consumed with growing desire. She was transported away from the memory of recent events, away from anything she'd ever experienced. Swept away with the magic of his touch, of his taste, of his caresses.

When he ended the kiss, she clung. Her lids were so heavy, she had to force them open, gazing into the deep, dark eyes of the man who still held her.

''The first kiss is always awkward. Better to have it in private than before an audience,'' he said.

Releasing her, he stooped to retrieve the nightgown that had dropped to the floor. He pressed it into her hands and then brushed her lips once with his thumb as if capturing some of the moisture to take with him.

Sara watched, dazed, as he spun around and left. The slight click when the door shut released her from the spell.

Dazed, she crossed slowly to the bed, sinking down on the edge, holding the nightgown against her breasts, feeling the softness of the material and the damp terry cloth of the towels.

The first kiss? Oh, Lord, there were going to be more?

CHAPTER THREE

WHEN Sara awoke the next morning, her first thought was of Kharun. Wouldn't that stroke his ego? But not in the way he might like. She'd spent a long time last night trying to figure a way out of this outlandish proposal of his. There had to be a way to scrape through with neither side losing.

Last evening before she slept, Aminna had brought her soup and salad and a soothing pot of tea. Once finished, Sara had slipped into bed, wishing for the oblivion of sleep. It proved elusive as she worried about today.

Her parents were the first obstacle. Or maybe Kharun's mother. Would she meet the ministers who questioned their relationship today? Have to defend herself to them? Show them how much she loved Kharun? A man she'd met less than twenty-four hours ago.

How about his sister, or his trusted adviser, Piers?

She pulled the sheet over her head, wishing she could go back to sleep and not wake up until the leases had been signed. The day loomed ahead, overwhelming and terrifying. They'd never pull this off!

But the scent of the sea beckoned. Long moments later she threw back the covers, rising to pad over to the wide-open French doors. The veranda was covered, sheltered from the morning sun. A narrow width of sunshine still warmed the tiles near the edge. Soon it would be gone. She stepped out, feeling the coolness of the tile gradually warm beneath her bare feet.

The breeze swirled the nightgown around her and she raised her head, letting the air brush through her hair. She wanted to go swimming, splash in the warmth of the Mediterranean, forget for a little while the mess she'd made of things.

But she couldn't. She had first to face the day. She turned and reentered her room. On the chaise longue near the door were her clothes—washed and neatly pressed. Sighing softly, she fetched them and headed for the bathroom. It was time to face reality.

Dressed, hair brushed, and wishing for some makeup, Sara entered the hallway and walked toward the entryway. She heard the murmur of voices, the clink of silver against china. Following the sound, she reached the dining room. It faced away from the sea. The French doors in this room opened to a garden. Riotous flowers bloomed everywhere—bright yellows, rich reds, and a waterfall of white blossoms, all contrasting with the deep green of leaves and stems.

The scent mingled with that of fresh-baked croissants and heavenly coffee.

Kharun sat at the head of the table, an older woman to his right. She was dressed in a fashionable dress of French design. The pearls around her neck and in her earrings were understated, but undoubtedly worth a fortune. She caught sight of Sara and paused, coffee cup raised halfway to her lips.

Kharun looked up.

''Sara, I thought you'd sleep in longer or we would

have waited." He rose and came to the doorway, capturing her hand in his. Raising it to his lips, he pressed a kiss upon her soft skin, his eyes catching hers—narrowed in warning.

"Good morning." The tone was intimate, the look one of possession and desire.

All resolve fled. What was it about this man that had her reacting like some teenager when the captain of the football team noticed her?

He switched to French. "May I present my mother, Angelique bak Samin? *Ma mère,* this is Sara Kinsale, my bride-to-be."

She arose to join them and gave Sara a kiss on each cheek.

"*Enchantée, mademoiselle.* My son was just telling me of your betrothal. I know you kept it a secret because of my husband's recent death, but such happy news deserves its time in the sun. It will lift the gloom that settles on our family. Welcome. You may call me Angelique."

Next to the two of them, Sara felt frumpy and awkward. She wished she had something to wear beside the khaki safari outfit she had thought so dashing only a few days ago.

"I am happy to meet you," she replied in French. At least she'd get some practice out of her expertise in the language.

What else would Kharun wish to practice? she wondered as he solicitously seated her at his left hand and summoned Aminna to bring a new pot of coffee.

"Tell me all about this whirlwind courtship. I was beginning to worry about my son. He has been so consumed with business since his father put him in charge. Now I'm pleased to know he is also taking time to assure his future and that of the family. You have brought joy to my heart."

Sara smiled awkwardly, feeling guilty as sin, grateful when Aminna arrived with the coffee. She stalled, making a great to-do of preparing the beverage to her liking. Please let something happen to deflect the inquisition, she prayed. She looked at Kharun for help. He got them into this particular situation, he could get them out!

Despite her worry, breakfast proceeded without a hitch. Kharun did indeed get them out of the awkwardness, regaling his mother with the most fantastic tale of how they met. Sara listened spellbound, hoping she could remember every word in case she was asked. It would prove smoother sailing if their stories matched.

By the time breakfast was over, Sara almost believed the fantasy herself—how they met in Paris, fell in love on the Rue de Calais, danced until dawn on the Left Bank, and learned more about each other strolling in the gardens of the Tulleries.

"I had planned to visit for a while," Angelique said. "But I will move immediately to Jasmine's apartment. You two will wish to be alone. Especially if you cannot take a proper honeymoon at this time. Kharun explained that once the oil leases are signed, he'd be able to take time. You are very understanding to allow the delay."

Sara blinked, her gaze moving to Kharun. What had he been telling his mother before she arrived? She smiled, wondering what she was supposed to say. She hadn't been a good actress when she had lines to memorize. Improvisation was even more difficult!

"We would not cut short your visit, Mother," he said.

"Nonsense, I remember how your father and I were—" Tears welled in her eyes and she blotted them with her linen napkin. She pushed back her chair. "Excuse me. I will instruct one of the maids to begin packing immediately." She left the room almost at a run.

"She should stay," Sara said, looking after her. "It's not like she'd interrupt anything."

"She and my father had a passionate love affair from the moment they met. I suspect she considers our situation similar. It's the only way she would have understood an immediate wedding."

Having experienced one of Kharun's kisses, she had no trouble instantly imagining them in a passionate embrace, ignoring the world around them, caught up in the splendor and excitement of touch and feelings and passion. What would it be like to be loved by this man?

But what he'd just said suddenly hit her. "*Immediate* wedding?"

"The sooner the better. Are you almost finished?"

She gulped the last of her coffee, blotted her lips with her napkin and laid it neatly on the table. Thoughts about Kharun were the last thing she needed. If she was to get through this charade, she needed her wits about her—not be daydreaming.

"I'm ready," she said.

"It's early yet. We have time."

"It's never too early at a hotel—they're open twenty-four hours."

"What do you mean?"

"You said you'd take me to the Presentation Hotel this morning. I'm ready."

"After our wedding." He looked at his watch, then met her stunned gaze. "Which is scheduled for ten. I think Jasmine has found you a suitable dress."

"*What?*"

He rose and was gone before she could formulate a coherent sentence. She followed him from the room with her gaze, stunned at the announcement. He couldn't have been serious! She couldn't marry him *this* morning. Weddings took tons of planning. Invitations and fittings and…and… She didn't know what else, having never married before. But she didn't think you could schedule a wedding with no more than twelve hours' notice. And without telling the bride first.

She jumped up, intent on finding him and telling him why they couldn't marry today. A few hours away from that awful jail and she'd begun to think of alternative scenarios that would let them off the hook. She had to find Kharun and offer different ideas before this one got out of hand.

As she walked into the entryway searching for her reluctant host, the front door opened and a petite, slender young woman entered, wearing a lovely rose-colored silk suit. Accompanying her was a tall man dressed in a chauffeur's uniform carrying a garment bag over one arm. The woman's dark hair gleamed in the sunshine looking almost blue-black. The two of them stared at each other for a moment.

"You must be Sara," the woman said in flawless English.

"Jasmine, I presume," Sara guessed. The woman looked like a small, feminine version of Kharun.

The sunny smile that broke out was a surprise. Jasmine nodded, studying Sara. "No wonder my brother said yes to that crazy spur-of-the-moment idea."

"It'll never work," Sara said.

"If Kharun says it will, it will. I have brought your wedding dress." She flicked a glance to the man standing beside her. "Which room did Aminna give you?"

"Down there," Sara indicated. "But—"

Jasmine took the garment bag from the chauffeur and dismissed him. She turned to head for Sara's room.

"Quickly, you need to try it on. It wasn't easy to get something in your size on a moment's notice. Kharun called me at seven this morning asking if I would pick up a wedding dress. Doesn't he know most boutiques don't open before ten? Silly question, of course he doesn't. Let's see if this fits."

Sara followed, feeling swept away by a whirlwind.

Twenty minutes later Sara stared at her reflection in the floor-length mirror. Everything was spinning out of control. She hadn't found Kharun, but had been bustled along with Jasmine, coerced into trying on the gown. The creamy-white dress fit as if it had been made for her, lacy and elegant—suitable for cocktails, a trip to the theater, or a morning wedding. The shoes were a size too big, but Jasmine had already stuffed cotton in the toes, and they were low-heeled enough to manage.

Sara's blond curls encircled her head like a soft cloud.

The light touch of makeup Jasmine brought enhanced every feature, deepening the mysterious look of her eyes, bringing a hint of blush to her cheeks—making her look almost like a bride.

What would Kharun think?

At least she looked one hundred times better than when he'd first met her—when he'd made his proposal. Surely he could find no fault with the end result.

Slowly, Sara smiled. She liked how she looked. Maybe, just maybe, people wouldn't wonder what he saw in her. Maybe they could pull this off. For the sake of her father she had to try.

Jasmine met her gaze in the mirror, her expression solemn. "Bring no disgrace on my family. Do no harm to Kharun. Do you understand?"

Sara raised her chin and glared at Jasmine. "I would never do that. Nor bring disgrace to my family—isn't that the entire reason for this charade?"

In those short words, reality returned. She was not a blushing bride going to exchange vows with the man she loved. She was entering into a marriage of convenience—not even her convenience—to rectify a mistake. She would not compound it by forgetting for one second why the marriage was taking place.

Taking a discreet peek at her watch, she realized if the wedding was to begin at ten, she had no time to find Kharun and propose her alternative suggestions. It didn't matter, she knew he would never have accepted her ideas. The time for deciding had long passed.

This could work. Once the leases were signed, they'd

get an annulment and go their separate ways. She could do this. It was only for a few weeks.

Kharun left nothing to chance. He arranged for Samuel Kinsale and his wife to attend the ceremony. To do less might raise suspicions. But he timed their arrival to just minutes before he planned to start. They could visit with their daughter after she was legally his wife.

His mother and sister, of course, would attend. His most trusted adviser, Piers. He did not send an invitation to his aunt and uncle. He wouldn't risk their disrupting the ceremony before it could begin. Being a family in mourning helped. A quiet ceremony would be all that was expected.

Promptly at ten, Samuel Kinsale and his wife Roberta arrived. Angelique greeted them and led the way to the garden nearest the sea. She answered their questions as best she could, but Samuel wasn't satisfied. He and his wife had no indication their youngest even knew Kharun, much less planned to marry him, until that morning when Kharun had phoned. And the explanations had been hasty and brief.

Angelique told him what she knew and urged them to await to question Sara until after the ceremony.

The garden was the perfect setting for a quiet, family wedding. Kharun cynically reviewed everything from his place at the doorway. On the surface the locale presented as romantic a picture as he could devise. As long as no one questioned them closely, or challenged anything, it should go off without a hitch. Kinsale remained a question mark. He hoped the man would listen to Angelique and not question Sara until after the ceremony.

Sara was also an unknown. Would she go through with the bargain? Or would she defect at the last moment—thus giving Garh and his associates a weapon to use in their mind-set against progress?

Jasmine hurried down the hall and smiled uncertainly at her brother.

"She's as ready as I can make her. Good luck, brother. I still think an engagement would have worked."

"Sit with mother, she's a bit overwhelmed."

"I don't blame her. How is the bride's family taking it?"

He glanced out to the garden, frowning slightly. "Better than I expected, actually, though her mother looks shell-shocked. Her father put up a fuss when he first arrived, but seems content with waiting to talk to Sara later. I wonder if he had already heard the rumors? He would appreciate the need for such a step."

"Maybe they're glad to get her off their hands," she murmured as she slipped past on her way to join the others.

He turned and waited until he saw Sara walking down the hall. For a moment Kharun forgot they were entering into a marriage for business necessity. His bride appeared entirely different from anytime he'd seen her—including earlier that morning.

He almost caught his breath. She looked shy, virginal and breathtakingly lovely. There would be few questions asked when his uncle's ministers saw her. They'd immediately conclude the reasons why he was marrying her—for her looks, her mind and her background.

"Are my folks here?" she asked, stepping up to the doorway.

"Everyone is gathered in the garden. Are you ready?"

She hesitated a moment, then nodded.

"Then?" He held out his arm.

She took his elbow, gripping tightly. "Shouldn't my father walk me down the aisle?"

"It is a very informal wedding—only immediate family. I don't think we need stand on protocol."

"Or you don't trust me alone with him before?" she whispered as they stepped into the sunshine. She'd given her word of honor. He might not think much of it given the circumstances, but it meant a lot to her. She smiled at her parents, but continued to hold on to Kharun. She'd set this in motion, she'd see it through. Better her family thought she was rushing into marriage than to learn the truth. When it didn't last, they probably wouldn't be surprised.

Maybe one day, after her father finalized the deal, she'd tell them the whole story.

But not today. Today she was getting married in a lovely garden, with the Mediterranean Sea in the background, to a man who could have been a dream come true—but might prove to be her worst nightmare.

Sara knew the day would forever be etched in her memory as a series of sketches. From the fragrance of the flowers surrounding her while she took vows, to the hot demanding kiss Kharun had given to seal their marriage, to the bewildered look of her mother when she turned to hug her. Both her parents had pulled her aside as soon as the short receiving line ended and questioned her about the totally unexpected wedding.

Sara had her history of impetuousness to stand her in good stead. They were not surprised by anything she did anymore, so accepted the fact she and Kharun had decided to marry after a whirlwind courtship. Her mother had questions galore, but Sara staved her off, promising to visit soon and let her know all the details. Her fingers had been firmly crossed behind her back and she hoped the need for the charade would end before her mother cornered her!

The wedding lunch had been extravagant—as if the staff had had weeks to prepare instead of less than twelve hours. The conversation on the other hand, had proved stilted and awkward as Kharun's family, except for Jasmine, did not speak English, and Samuel and Roberta Kinsale didn't speak Arabic. Her father did have a limited command of French, so there was some conversation between him and Angelique.

It had been a strain—pretending to be a blushing bride, all the time conscious of the man beside her. Of his fingertips brushing against hers, which sent jolts of electricity shooting in every direction. Of the intensity of his gaze—which the others had taken as devotion, but Sara knew was more of an assessment, and warning to keep to their deception.

The trip to the hotel to gather her clothes later that afternoon had been accomplished with no fuss. Kharun never left her side. She knew he didn't trust her, but to anyone else, it looked as if he were a devoted bridegroom who couldn't bear to be parted from his beloved.

The oddest memory was of the confused feelings she'd experienced when Kharun had bid her good-night and left her in the middle of the living room.

By then everyone had left—including Aminna. Only she and Kharun remained in the villa. Aminna would return in two days—it was all Kharun had asked for a honeymoon, alluding to a longer one when the demands of his time were less immediate.

She might as well be alone in the world, Sara thought as she listened for some sound. Once his footsteps faded, she heard nothing except the soft soughing of the sea breeze and the rustle of the curtains as they moved with the wind.

She went to her bedroom and closed the door. Within minutes she was nestled in bed, with a magazine she'd seen earlier in hand. But her thoughts were not on the pages.

She'd never thought about getting married—not for years. And certainly not to prevent an international scandal. But being alone in a big bed was never her fantasy for her wedding night. She was disappointed Kharun had not spent more time with her. Sending away the staff had been brilliant—no one around to see they were not the lovers everyone suspected.

But for a moment, she almost wished he'd taken advantage of his right to share her bed. Shocked at the idea, she clicked off the light, letting the magazine slide to the floor as she scooted down on the bed. Her last

thought as she finally drifted to sleep was that she hoped
the business talks would conclude soon.

Sara awoke early the next morning, having slept better
than she expected. She dressed quickly in a sundress
she'd brought and wandered out onto the veranda. The
sun was already warming the day. The sea sparkled beneath its rays, looking cool and inviting. She followed
the path that led through the gardens to the beach. A
quick glance around assured her she was alone. The servants wouldn't return until late tomorrow afternoon.
Where was Kharun? Still asleep?

The image of him in a bed flashed into her mind. He'd
need a big bed. Would he sprawl across it, taking up all
the room, or keep to the edge as if ready to leap up in
a second's notice? Did he sleep in anything?

She doubted it.

The thought brought tantalizing new images to mind.
Trying to block them out of her mind, she opened the
low gate to the sand. Sara kicked off her sandals and
walked on the hot surface. Running quickly to the water's edge, she almost danced in relief as the cool sea
lapped at her feet. Looking left and then right, she saw
she was alone. She tried to imagine such a pristine lo-
cation being empty in America—impossible. Every time
she'd gone to the beach, she'd had to share it with families and couples and teenagers. Today's solitude was
blissful.

She began to walk along the water's edge.

When she reached a notice board, written in Arabic,
she turned around. Maybe that was the edge of Kharun's

property. She'd ask, but in the meantime, she was growing hungry. Longingly, she gazed at the water. She
wanted to swim, but knew she needed someone else at
hand. Maybe later. Turning, she headed for the villa.

She brushed her feet off when she reached the gate
and donned her sandals again. Walking through the gardens, she wondered if it would be okay to pick some of
the blossoms to carry to her room. They were so lovely
and fragrant, she'd enjoy them where she could see
them.

She entered her bedroom, crossing to the hallway. It
was the only way she knew to reach the dining room.
Maybe she'd spend some time today exploring the villa.
If she had to live here for a few weeks, she might as
well know the layout.

Just as she reached the entryway, a loud knock
sounded on the door. Sara hesitated. Should she see who
it was, or wait for Kharun? There was no one else to
answer.

The knock sounded again.

Sara opened the door and saw an elderly woman
dressed all in black. Her gray hair was pulled tightly
back in a bun. Her skin was wrinkled, no makeup soft-
ened the aging process. Her eyes snapped when she
looked at Sara. Her gaze ran from head to toe and then
back.

Beyond her sat a huge old car. The chauffeur stood
near the front, watching the scene impassively.

The woman said something.

"I hope you speak English or French, because I don't

speak Arabic,'' Sara said. Then repeated the sentence in French.

The woman responded in that language.

"The wife of a sheikh should at least speak his language,'' she snapped. "Are you going to invite me in?''

"Please,'' Sara said, stepping aside, wondering who in the world the woman was.

"I suppose it's too much to expect my nephew to inform his uncle and me when he weds. Just like him to ignore family in his pursuit of his own ways. I have told Hamsid, but does he listen? No. Just like a man!''

Sara watched the woman—obviously Kharun's aunt. Had he mentioned her to Sara?

"Well, where is he?'' she snapped, glaring at Sara.

"Kharun?'' Sara ventured.

"Of course, who else?'' The woman peered at her as if she were daft.

Sara looked around, hoping inspiration would strike. She knew the circumstances surrounding their marriage were top secret. But everyone would expect a new wife to know where her husband of less than twenty-four hours was.

"Um, I'll go get him,'' she said. "Would you like to wait—''

"I'm not going traipsing all through the place to find him. Where are the servants?''

"They were given a few days off. So we could be alone.''

"Then hurry up.''

Sara turned toward the dining room, almost skipping in her haste. She hoped she could find Kharun, and prayed he hadn't left. What would she do if she had to return and tell the woman he had gone out?

How many rooms did the house have? she wondered five minutes later. She'd tried every door she'd come across. Some of the rooms looked lived in, others like showplaces. But all were empty of human life.

Sara stopped and wanted to scream. The impatient woman was waiting. She had no idea where her husband was, nor what she was going to do next. How dare he put her in this position!

Slowly she retraced her steps, heading for the entryway. If she had any luck, the woman would have tired and left.

The sound of voices alerted her to the fact Kharun had found their guest. Thank goodness!

She drew a deep breath and hurried to join them.

Kharun and his aunt didn't notice Sara slipping into the room, they were too busy arguing. She didn't understand a word, but she understood the anger in their tones, and the hard glares they exchanged.

Suddenly Kharun saw Sara. He stopped talking and smiled.

Sara's heart caught then turned a slow, lazy somersault. It was the first time she'd seen him smile at her. She'd thought him handsome when she'd first seen him, but his smile almost stopped her heart. The man should be labeled as a lethal weapon and a warning issued to all females under the age of ninety-eight!

Caught in his gaze, she walked slowly toward him, her skin tingling with awareness and the potent attraction any woman feels around a stunningly masculine male.

He wasn't wearing a suit, she noticed dimly. His shirt was loose, buttoned only partway up, exposing a wedge of broad tanned chest sprinkled with dark hair. His hair was mussed, as if he'd run his fingers through it while working. Or as if tossed by the sea breeze. Had he walked along the shore today, as well?

His trousers were loose and he was barefooted—his feet planted firmly on the floor as if boldly staking his claim and asserting to the world he was totally, completely male—ready to take on all comers. She swallowed hard, amazed to realize this man was her husband.

"Ah, Sara, I wondered where you were." His voice was sultry, sensuous. His eyes caressed her. His hand reached for hers, drawing her closer, his fingers tightening in warning as he pulled her close enough she felt the heat pouring from his body.

Mesmerized, she could not say a word, but her senses seemed to be on overdrive. Every nuance was clear, dazzling. His fingers holding hers were warm and strong. His eyes tried to convey a message, but she wasn't sure what he wanted.

Until he swept her into his arms and kissed her.

She didn't know this man, wasn't sure she even liked him. His kiss meant nothing—merely show for an audience of one.

But one touch and she felt afloat on a sea of sensation and delight. Bright colors kaleidoscoped behind her lids. Her blood seemed to heat until she wondered if it would evaporate. Her senses swam with delight, with shimmering pleasure.

When his tongue stroked her lips, she parted them.

When it danced in her mouth, she met each foray with a caress of her own. When he deepened the kiss, she pressed against the length of his hard body, shocked with the reaction she was causing. But it wasn't enough. She wanted more.

A harsh exclamation behind her slowly penetrated. Kharun eased back, breathing hard as he gazed down into her eyes, his own shuttered and impossible to read.

He placed his arm on Sara's shoulders and turned her into his body, still holding her as he spoke in French, "What did you expect, Aunt. Sara and I haven't seen each other for months. We are married and don't have time for a honeymoon. We will make our own, here, and with every moment we can spare."

"I do not understand this. Take your honeymoon, there is nothing that cannot wait."

"You forget the oil leases I'm negotiating."

"Bah, you are foolish if you think you will garner the ministers' approval. Your uncle indulges you foolishly. But the treaty has not been signed yet."

"We have discovered a new reserve, a huge one, that will enable us to make deals for years to come. The new influx of cash will enable changes, improvements. Bring us into the twenty-first century."

"Your father—"

"Unfortunately he is dead. Out of deference to our mourning, Sara and I had a quiet ceremony yesterday. Mother and Jasmine represented our family. Sara had her own parents present. When our mourning time is passed, we will have a public reception and you may formally welcome Sara into our family."

The woman glared at Sara. She spoke again in Arabic. Kharun tightened his hold, his eyes blazing with anger. He responded in the language then disengaged himself from Sara and headed for the door.

In a very polite voice, he bid his aunt farewell.

When he shut the door behind her, he spun around and looked at Sara.

"That went well."

"That went well?" she exclaimed. "I didn't understand a word of what she said, but I didn't need to. Her tone of voice spoke volumes!"

"Ah, but she never once suspected this as a coverup. She deplored my choice of brides, warned me to keep a tight rein lest you ruin us all, and railed against me for defying the ministers who have more experience in deciding things than I do. But not once did she act as if she didn't believe the marriage."

CHAPTER FOUR

"IF SHE thought about it for two seconds, she might have," Sara mumbled, annoyed Kharun seemed so pleased with himself.

"Why?" He focused his attention on her.

Sara almost shivered, the memory of that hot kiss sending heat washing through her. He was an intense man, and when he turned that intensity on her, she felt like she was the only person in the world.

"I didn't know where you were, nor how to find you. If you hadn't wandered in on your own, I'd be making up some sort of excuse as to why a bride didn't know where her bridegroom was twenty-four hours after the wedding!"

He nodded. "Good point. Come with me, I will show you around the villa and how to use the intercom system. When Aminna is here, she can always find me. Or one of the maids."

"She'll be back tomorrow. If we don't have any more unexpected guests, I don't need a tour." She couldn't explain her reluctance to spend time with Kharun. They meant nothing to each other, yet he kissed her as if she were his passion. And she responded like a firecracker.

False passion—he turned off the charm instantly when they were alone. Although not quite. Just standing there had her fantasizing about things that could never be. He made no effort to entice her. To him their arrangement was pure expediency to keep scandal from tainting his negotiations. But he didn't have to do anything, but stand there and she was captivated. She looked away, trying to get her wayward emotions under some sort of control.

"Come and see the villa anyway. My mother decorated it over the years. I urged her to take some of the furnishings or paintings for her own apartment when she left after my father's death, but she says the memories become too strong and too sad."

For one foolish moment, Sara wished he'd held out his hand when urging her to come on the tour. She would love to slip her hand into his to feel his strength, to feel anchored. To revel in the shimmering waves of tingling awareness that would shoot up her arm at his touch. To relish his touch, and fantasize a bit more before reality returned.

She frowned as she stepped toward the arched hallway. Where had that last thought come from? She didn't want to be anchored, and she didn't need fantasy in her life.

She was a free spirit, hadn't her parents lamented that fact for years? She still had to make her way in the world and show her parents she could accomplish something worthwhile as her siblings had.

"Do you have my camera, Kharun?" she asked as they walked down the corridor opposite the one that led to her bedroom.

"Planning to complete your assignment?" he asked warily.

She flushed slightly. "No. But it was an expensive piece of equipment."

He paused by an open doorway. It was an office, set up with high-tech communications equipment, two computers, an enormous desk, and rows of bookshelves along one wall. French doors opened to the wrap-around veranda and allowed the cool breeze to waft in.

"It's in here."

On the corner of the desk sat the camera.

She stepped warily inside the office and went to pick it up, checking the exposure indicator. Reset to zero.

"The film was confiscated," he said, leaning against the doorjamb.

"I expected nothing else. Can I have some more?"

"To do what?"

"Exactly what I asked myself earlier," she said, swinging around and leaning against his desk. It was easier to face him with the width of the office between them. "What am I to do all day?"

"What do you do at home?"

"I have a job, so I show up at the office, scout around for new stories. There's shopping to do, friends to meet, laundry, household chores."

He raised an eyebrow. "Do you cook?"

She nodded.

"Since Aminna is not here, maybe you'd like to prepare some food for us."

"I don't suppose sheikhs learn to cook."

"Your assumption is flawed. I was on my own several times—when away at school. I can cook enough to get by when a restaurant isn't convenient."

"And a restaurant isn't convenient today?" Sara asked.

He slowly smiled and shook his head.

Her heart turned over. Her knees grew weak and she thought she'd have to learn to breathe all over again. She had already thought he was a striking specimen of alpha male, dominating any situation he was in, but when he smiled, he was devastating. If he didn't already have a calling, she knew he'd be an instant hit in Hollywood, or on the London stage.

She tried to hide her reactions. "So that gives me something to do today, what about the rest of the time while you're off negotiating oil leases and running a company?"

"We can work on that. It may only be a matter of weeks. Pretend you are on vacation. Enjoy the beach, you love the sea. Maybe go shopping. Come, I'll show you the rest of the villa and then you can prepare lunch for us."

She picked up the camera and looked around the room. "This is command central, I suppose?"

"It is my office at home. As you know I have formal offices in Staboul. But when I'm not there, I still need instant communication and access to my advisers. Unless I am present, please do not enter this room." His voice hardened with the last command.

She tilted her chin and glared at him. "I told you once before, I am not a spy. Anyway, I don't speak Arabic, so any secrets you had would be safe from me. I have no interest in your dumb old office." She swept toward him with as much dignity as she could muster beneath the smoldering anger. What would it take to convince the man she was only a sometimes inept novice reporter for a second-rate U.S. tabloid and not a sexy, conniving spy?

Not that the sexy spy role didn't have advantages, she thought as he stepped aside to allow her into the hall. Weren't sexy spies notorious for seducing secrets from lots of men? For a moment Sara wondered if she had the capability to seduce Kharun.

The tour took more than an hour. She was impressed with the comfort level of the villa despite the antiques and costly items that predominated. The paintings on the walls were originals. Her favorite room was the one where Matisse paintings dominated an entire wall. She knew she'd come back on her own just to soak up the ambience.

There were formal rooms, a quiet little sunroom, guest rooms for both family and visitors. Even an exercise room tucked in a back corner. On the far side of the villa was a pool, surrounded by fragrant flowering shrubs, which provided privacy.

"Why have a pool when the Mediterranean Sea is at your doorstep?" she asked when they entered the pool area.

"Some people prefer artificial to natural." He shrugged. "Here we have both. You are free to use either—provided you don't go swimming alone."

"Who would go with me?"

"If I am available, I will go. Otherwise Aminna or one of the maids or gardeners can watch to make sure you don't get into trouble."

"Afraid I'll swim away?" she asked lightly.

"No, Sara, afraid solely for your well-being. It is not safe to swim alone."

She nodded, suddenly touched he'd extend his concern to her well-being after the trouble she'd caused. He was right, it was unsafe to swim alone.

Kharun ended the tour in the kitchen. Sara stared in amazement. "You must entertain a lot," she murmured, taking in the huge stainless-steel refrigeration unit, the industrial-size gas range, the two huge ovens and three microwave ovens. The counter space would provide enough room to cater a seven-course meal for fifty.

"My parents did a lot of entertaining. I don't do as much. Though now that we are married, I wonder if it will become expected."

"No."

"No?" He looked at her. "Why not?"

"I'm not good at gatherings like that," she said quickly. "Besides, we won't be married that long. No one would expect us to entertain."

"Why are you not good at gatherings?"

"I never know what to say to people. We've been involved with big receptions my whole life. You must know that most business deals are often dealt with at social functions. I never told my father, but I hate going to them. One wrong word and world peace as we know it could end."

Kharun laughed out loud. Sara watched him, fascinated. Her lips twitched, but even his laugher couldn't erase the awkward feelings she got when faced with a roomful of strangers.

"It's not funny," she said.

He came to stand next to her—too close. She wanted to step away. She could feel the heat from his body as it seemed to envelop her, smell the scent from his skin that had her wanting to toss her camera to the floor and draw an enticing finger along the swell of his muscles to test their strength, taste him again.

She swallowed and stood her ground, hoping her pounding heartbeat wasn't evident to the astute man now staring down into her eyes.

"It is not funny, I apologize for laughing. But any faux pas you might make at a reception or dinner would scarcely end world peace. If you are uncomfortable, we will not entertain."

She blinked. That was totally unexpected. "It's your home, if you wish to entertain, I'll do my best. Just understand I'm not so great at it. Now, Margaret, she shines at events like that. She knows just what to say, who're the most important people in the room, what the latest rumors are and how to defuse any awkward situations."

"Margaret, is she your sister?"

Sara nodded. "The attorney," she said flatly.

"Ah, I remember now, the attorney and the physicist and the...photographer."

"Photojournalist, this week." Unless her boss had already fired her. She hadn't reported in for a week. She looked at Kharun, trying to gauge his reaction if she asked to use the phone.

"I probably should let my office know what's happened."

He shrugged. "If they are any kind of newspaper, they

already know. My office released news of our marriage this morning. I have cut off the phones to make sure we are not disturbed by reporters. My advisers will handle the world press.''

"Oh. It must be nice to have a legion of people ready to do your bidding."

He smiled as if amused by her comment. "It is. Lunch?"

Glancing around the room again, Sara nodded. She placed her camera on the edge of the counter and started opening cupboard doors, looking for something to start with. "So I join the legions, here for your bidding."

"Unless you wish to starve." Humor laced his tone.

She ignored him. When she reached the refrigeration unit, she was delighted to see a bowl of freshly cleaned and boiled shrimp. Had Aminna suspected they'd like something like that for lunch? "I can make a shrimp salad for lunch, will that work?"

"Fine. I'll be back in twenty minutes. Does that give you enough time?"

"Sure." The image of the two of them working intimately together in the kitchen vanished. So much for thinking it a way to get to know her husband better.

Temporary husband! Their marriage was a business arrangement, nothing more, she admonished herself as she drew things from the shelves. She didn't want to be here any more than he wanted her here. She wanted to be out proving herself to her family. To show she could find a niche and make a career.

Sara sighed softly. Photojournalism wasn't it, she admitted to herself. She wasn't exactly sure what was, but there was no use kidding herself. She was washed up as a hot-shot reporter—even before she wrote her first big story, too.

Sometimes life wasn't fair.

She loaded a large tray she'd found with the salads, freshly cut French bread, and glasses of a cola she'd found in the refrigerator. Carrying it carefully, she made her way to the terrace beside the sparkling pool. There was shade in the far side and a table conveniently at hand.

Setting the small table, she was pleased with the way lunch had turned out. Now to figure out how to get Kharun out here to eat.

"It looks good."

She jumped at his voice. He'd come up behind her without making a sound.

"Aminna had all the ingredients, it was easy to throw together."

He seated her and sat opposite. She was pleased to note after the first hesitant bite, that he dug in with enthusiasm. She tasted the shrimp salad, pleased at how tasty it was.

Kharun obliquely studied his new bride as they ate. She seemed to pulse with restless energy, looking around her with fresh eyes, smiling in pleasure at the flowers that bloomed near the pool. She seemed to love beauty. He had noticed that as they'd toured the villa. What other interests did this stranger bound to him have?

"I have work to do this afternoon. At five, however, I plan to go riding. Would you care to join me?" he asked out of the blue. He rarely let others accompany him riding—that was his time for himself. Generally in a hectic week if he could carve out a couple of hours for himself, he guarded the time. Why had he invited Sara to join him?

"I'd love to. Where would we ride?"

"Along the beach. Normally I keep Satin in a stable a few miles from the city. I like to ride in the desert at dusk. But I brought him here a couple of weeks ago. It's not quite the same thing, but a good ride."

"How far can we go before we run into people sunbathing or swimming?"

"If we head away from Staboul, we can go for several miles. In the opposite direction—toward the city, only two. Do you have riding clothes?"

"I have jeans, that'll do for today. Who is Satin?"

"My horse. His Arabian name translates to Satin Magic. There are two other horses at the stables, I'll have one saddled for you. Do you prefer a spirited horse or one who is more sedate?"

"Spirited, of course. I want to ride like the wind along the sea."

Her eyes sparkled when she spoke, the gray going silver with delight. So it wasn't only anger that changed the color. Passion also brought out the silvery lights. What else did Sara feel passionately about?

He reined in his thoughts. An occasional kiss in public to maintain their charade was one thing. But this woman was a stranger, one who was here under obscure circumstances. There was no passion to be had between them.

Once the leases for the oil rights were finalized and signed, they would part ways.

He rose, tossing his napkin on the table. "Lunch was delicious. I'll come for you at five." He turned to walk away before he had second thoughts—on anything.

"Kharun?" She spoke before he reached the house.

"Yes?" He turned. She gathered their plates, stacking them on a tray.

"I wish to go swimming this afternoon. I'll use the pool. I'm sure I'll be okay if there's no one around."

He hesitated, but it was not an option. His young cousin had died when they'd been children—drowned in an accident that had burned deep into his consciousness.

"I'll bring my reading to the terrace while you swim," he said.

"Oh." She looked nonplussed. He almost smiled. She fascinated him, this Western woman with the changing eyes. "Give me half an hour."

"Sure, I have to clean up and change and all. That's fine. Thanks." She began humming as she swept the last of the breadcrumbs from the table into her hand, dumping them into one of the used plates.

From jail cell to luxury—Sara seemed to fit into both with a built-in self-sufficiency.

As he headed for his office, he remembered her comment about being uncomfortable at formal gatherings. It was too bad she felt that way. He bet she'd keep people on their toes and intrigue them to boot.

It was forty-five minutes later when Kharun stepped back onto the terrace. He had brought his laptop, and a stack of folders to skim through. Sara was sitting on the side of the pool, dangling her feet in the water.

For the first time, he was glad he'd worn his sunglasses. He hoped they disguised his reaction to seeing her in that sleek swimsuit. Electric blue, it hugged her body. Her high, firm breasts were clearly displayed, as was her narrow waist and sweet flare of hips. Her legs went on forever when she stood and walked toward the deep end.

"Thanks for coming. I won't swim that long. Then I'll lie in the sun for a while and work on my tan."

He nodded and continued to the table where they'd shared lunch. It remained in the shade and he needed all the cooling he could find. His blood warmed at the sight of her. Desire rose. He had enjoyed kissing her, making the best of a bad situation.

Now he wanted her on another level, one that had nothing to do with their bargain or situation.

He wanted her in every way a man wants a woman.

Kharun set his chair so he could watch her without appearing to. She dove neatly into the water, coming up to begin swimming. Her legs kicked strongly, her arms rose and fell in a steady motion as she cleaved through the water. Turning at the end, she continued to swim. And he continued to watch. She was supple and graceful and strong. Obviously swimming was a sport she enjoyed—and excelled at. It proved a pleasure to watch her.

When at last she rose at the far end and sat on the edge, he looked away. But not before noticing how her breasts rose and fell as she tried to catch her breath.

How her wild curls were weighted down with water and hung like shining waves on either side of her face.

And not before he noticed his desire had increased, not diminished. He flipped open the laptop and clicked it on. He had work to do—and it definitely did not include fantasizing about his wife. His *temporary* wife.

Wife. They were married. Neither were promised to another. And weren't Western women supposed to be much more free with their favors than the women of his culture? Maybe he should explore that avenue a bit further.

He looked at Sara. Would she be willing to have an affair while she was here?

CHAPTER FIVE

SARA was ready at five for the promised ride. She'd donned sturdy shoes, comfortable jeans, and a sleeveless yellow top. The sun had kissed her skin at the pool, and she had a healthy glow about her.

She'd wondered earlier if Kharun would join her in the pool, but he'd diligently worked all afternoon—never looked up once as far as she could tell. She'd done some laps, rested on the side, and then swum some more before lying down on a sunbed at the water's edge.

He'd returned to the house once she'd told him she didn't plan to swim again. In fact, he had departed so fast she might have been insulted under other circumstances. Would it have hurt to stay a few moments and maybe talk?

She refused to let any vague feeling of disappointment color her excitement for the upcoming ride. She loved horses and had often wished she could have owned one. But with her father's constant travels when she was younger, and her own future uncertain lately, she had never felt the time was right.

How lucky for Kharun to have a stable close by. Riding along the beach sounded wildly romantic.

Romantic?

"Fun, I meant fun," she said out loud. "It'll be fun."

A light tap on her door startled her. "Great, now he'll

think I talk to myself,'' she mumbled as she hastened to the door.

"Ready?'' Kharun asked. He was also dressed casually, in light pants and high, glossy riding boots. His loose shirt would shelter him from the sun's rays, yet allow the wind to sweep through keeping him cool in the hot afternoon.

She smiled brightly. "I sure am.'' And glad to have a respite from being cooped up in the house, but she wouldn't tell him that. She was grateful, actually, for the opportunity to keep her embarrassing mistake from her father. She needed to act accordingly.

Obviously not all of the servants had been granted time off, there were several men working in the stables, which proved to be a short walk from the villa. Two Arabian horses were already saddled, standing in the shade near a water trough.

One was larger than the other, as black as midnight, with a long flowing mane and tail. The second horse was a bay with one white stocking dusting the left rear hoof.

"They're beautiful,'' Sara said, enchanted. She walked over to them and patted both on the neck. Fumbling in her pocket, she pulled out two carrots, which she fed to the well-mannered horses.

"A way to make a friend for life,'' Kharun said, watching her.

He stood nearby his feet spread slightly, his hands on his hips. He looked the epitome of wild desert sheikh. Instead of the lush greenery behind him, he should have had miles of golden desert sand, and the crystal blue of a vast and empty sky. Maybe tents to one side, with his trusty desert raiders with him.

Sara almost shivered in reaction. She was here to ride, not to fantasize.

"This must be Satin Magic," she said, patting the gleaming black horse once more. He was sleek and strong—the perfect mount for Kharun.

"And who is this?" she asked as she ran her hand along the neck of the bay.

"Alia. Don't let her docile air fool you. With a rider on her back, she expects to go places and runs like the wind."

"Sounds great."

"Then, if you are ready?"

Kharun held her waist and boosted her to the horse. Sara could have managed by herself, but kept quiet, savoring the tingling sensations where his hands were. He helped her adjust her stirrups, the brush of his arm and hands against her legs heating her blood more than the sun had.

"All set?" he asked, looking up at her.

"Yes." It came out far more breathless than she'd expected. Turning her horse, she waited for him to mount his.

In only moments they were walking the horses out of the stable yard and down a winding path toward the sea.

The Mediterranean sparkled in the late afternoon sunshine, a deep mysterious blue stretching as far as the eye could see. The brassy glare of the midday sun had mellowed as the sun sank lower in the western sky. Colors grew richer. The green of the grass and shrubs gave way to the white of the sand.

Alia seemed impatient, pulling a little on the bit, as if anxious to race along the water's edge. Sara wondered if the horse and she were in communion—that's exactly what she yearned to do, too. Race fast enough to escape her thoughts.

As soon as they reached the sand, the horse pranced.

"She's ready to run," Sara said, glancing at Kharun. He looked as if he'd been born to ride. His control of the powerful horse he rode seemed effortless, yet she knew it was a demonstration of his skill. Horse and rider looked perfect together.

"Then let's oblige her," he said with a sudden wicked grin. Without a visible sign, he gave his horse his head and Satin Magic stretched out into a controlled canter, sand kicking up behind him.

"We can't let them get ahead of us," Sara said as she urged Alia into a gallop, her own competitive instincts rising.

In seconds both horses were running neck and neck along the pristine beach, sand spraying behind the thundering hoofs. The breeze from the Mediterranean enhanced the feeling of speed as they let their horses set the pace. Sara laughed out loud, feeling wild and free. It was exhilarating! She felt as if she could ride forever. As if only the darkness of night could slow them down, and maybe not even then. Alia was a magical horse with a smooth gait and easy disposition. Sara was falling in love with her after only a few minutes. Could they ride every day?

The beach stretched out ahead of them, the blue of the water a blur to the right as the horses seemed to gallop for pure joy. Stretching their legs, bunching and shifting muscles, gaits smooth and synchronous, as if they'd matched strides a million times in the past and would that many more in the future.

Several minutes later Kharun slowed from a gallop to an easy canter. Sara followed suit. It was almost as exciting as a flat-out, go-for-broke run and easier on the horses. She watched where they were going, but had time to enjoy the remoteness of the beach, the cool breeze from the water, the splashes when an errant finger of water crossed their path and they plunged through.

Finally, in the distance, she began to see signs of others on the beach. Kharun motioned for her to slow down. She complied instantly, bringing Alia to a complete stop. Both she and her horse were breathing hard. Her blood pumped through her veins. She felt exhilarated, alive.

"That was fabulous!" she said when Kharun reined in beside her. "That's the public beach ahead, I take it?"

"Yes. We can continue for another half mile or so if you like, but at a much slower pace. I do not wish to take the horses where people are using the beach."

"Just a bit farther, then." She walked her horse and Kharun came along beside her, his knee almost brushing against hers. She could have reached out to touch him with no effort. She glanced his way.

His hair was tousled from their run, but he didn't appear to be having trouble catching his breath. He slid a look in her direction.

"You ride well."

"I told you, best lessons money could buy. I always wanted a horse, but talk about impractical with Dad's job and all."

"If you like, I can arrange for you to ride while you are here. As long as you are accompanied by a groom, of course," Kharun said.

"You're not very trusting. Do you think I'll just ride away and never return?"

He shrugged. "It wouldn't matter if you tried, I would come after you."

His words sent a shiver of awareness down her back. Of course he would. They had an agreement. But even beyond that—if she left, he would be humiliated before everyone. That would prove an even worse situation than the incident she almost caused by being caught taking illegal photographs.

"I wouldn't do that," she said.

"You would do nothing to jeopardize your father's career, right?" His voice held a mocking tone.

Sara flared up. "That's true. But that's not the only reason. I gave you my word, and that means something to me. As long as the situation is as it is, you have nothing to worry about with me, Kharun. I stand by my promises. I said I'd stay until the leases are signed and I will. I said I'd pretend this was a great marriage and I will. I've done nothing to give you cause to think otherwise!"

"It's still early days. Who knows what you might decide to do given the opportunity."

She could tell from his tone he was skeptical. She

chafed at the restrictions but reminded herself she'd brought it all on due to her impetuous actions. Time would show him she could be trusted.

But none of that mattered right now. The ride was not over. She'd enjoy each moment as it came.

So she could remember when she left?

The thought surprised her. Would she want memories about her marriage? It was a sham entered into solely to prevent a scandal.

She began to wonder what a marriage to Kharun would be like if it weren't a sham.

Would he follow his father's example and marry for passionate love? Or would he follow the dictates of his uncle's ministers and his aunt and marry for dynastic reasons?

Her own parents had a solid, loving marriage. But she didn't want to have a marriage like her mother's. Sara wanted to be a person in her own right, have her own interests and goals. Her own career.

Her mother was the perfect businessman's wife, loved to host parties, mingle with strangers, wear the right gown and always knew just what to do at the right time. Always knew the right thing to say.

As Kharun's wife would need to.

Sara sighed. It was hard to follow in such a paragon's steps.

"Why the sigh?" Kharun asked.

"What? Oh, I was thinking about my mother."

"She is a lovely woman. You will look as lovely when you are her age," he said.

She looked at him in startled surprise. "I will?"

He nodded once, abruptly.

"Thank you. That's one of the nicest compliments I've ever had." Made even more special coming from a man who didn't appear to like her, or trust her. "But Mom's a hard act to follow. She always knows what to say, what to wear, how to act."

"Perhaps that's her calling in life. She has made a niche for herself as your father's supporter. Somehow, I don't see you in a similar role."

Sara grinned at him. "Got it in one!"

"So what do you want to do in life, Sara Kinsale?"

Her grin faded. "I don't have a clue. That's what makes it so hard. My sister Margaret always knew she wanted to be an attorney from the day she started high school. Josh was scientific-minded from kindergarten, so they tell me. I know my parents despair of me ever settling down."

She didn't want to mention how pleased her mother had been that she married Kharun. She had to find something she was good at and pursue it. She had hoped the photojournalist job would be it. She had been taking pictures since she was little, and had a flare for it. But she'd blown her first major assignment.

"Did you always know you would one day run your family's business?" she asked.

He shook his head. "When I was growing up, I wanted to drive race cars, fly airplanes and pilot a submarine. But as I grew older, business fascinated me. Especially after my father let me work in various departments of the different family companies between school terms. I was hooked."

She was delighted to learn this tidbit about the serious man beside her. Who would have thought he once had frivolous ideas?

"So did you pursue any of those subjects in school? Maybe not piloting a submarine, but maybe racing?"

"Flying. I have a multi-engine license. But none of the others. By the time I was sent away to school, my father made it clear business acumen was important. So I focused my studies in that direction. My family has several interests that span shipping, manufacturing and exporting. That was the role I was groomed for."

"Did you want it?" she asked. Dynastic family responsibilities were beyond her experience.

"I find it much more challenging and rewarding than trying to garner the consensus of ministers each of whom seem to have their own agenda. My father loved that aspect."

"Do you have to run the companies? Can't you go back to your earlier dreams?"

"One cannot fight one's destiny. Surely you know that by now."

"Ouch." Was it her destiny to roam restlessly searching forever for some career that would hold meaning and interest?

Kharun drew up his horse. "Here is the path back to the stable. Have you had enough riding for today?"

"Yes. It's been great, but such a long time since I've been riding. My legs are a bit stiff already."

He led the way along the path until the stable came into view. Dismounting when the grooms ran out, Kharun tossed the reins to one of the men.

Sara slid off her horse before Kharun could come around to help her and smiled at the groom who took the reins.

"Whoa," she said, as she took a step and felt her legs fold up beneath her. Before she could hit the ground, however, Kharun's arms were around her, beneath her knees, behind her back. In one swoop he picked her up and held her against his chest.

"I can walk," she protested, leaning just a little into his masculine strength. Of course she could walk, but what woman in the world had never fantasized about some dashing, romantic man sweeping her off her feet and into his arms?

"Your legs will feel wobbly for a while. Sit and rest." He set her on a bench near the side of the stable.

Sara blinked. She had visions of Kharun carrying her through the flower-scented garden, through the opened French doors to her bedroom and—

Get a grip, she told herself, feeling the heat of embarrassment sweep up her cheeks.

"You're right, I'll be fine in a minute." She couldn't look at him. What if he suspected where her wild thoughts were running? Theirs was a contrived marriage, lasting only as long as the treaty negotiations. There were no romantic overtones, no enduring emotions between them.

But for a moment, Sara didn't think there had to be. They were married. He had kissed her a couple of times already. She looked up at him, her eyes focused on his mouth. She wanted more from him. And she suspected he wouldn't turn her down. What would happen if she kissed him?

Kharun was sitting at his desk in the study the next morning when Piers knocked on the open door and stuck his head in.

"Got a moment?" he asked. "I took a chance and came by to bring you the latest proposals."

"Piers. I wondered if you'd drop by this morning. Come in." Kharun put down the report he was reading and motioned his long-time friend and most trusted adviser to enter.

"Honeymoon over?" Piers asked, grinning at his friend. He carried his briefcase over to the desk and placed it in a cleared area, then sat in his usual spot.

"Such as it was."

"And?"

"Not that it's any of your business, but it's more difficult being married than I had anticipated."

"An engagement would have been better."

"But probably would not have fooled Garh, Hamin and the others."

Piers laughed. "A hastily planned ceremony doesn't make a marriage."

"It's binding enough."

"True, but an annulment will be easy once the negotiations are finished." He opened his briefcase and pulled out a folder. "The latest from Samuel Kinsale. Do you think he is mellowing because his daughter married you? It seems we may be able to close the deal sooner than anticipated."

Kharun looked up at that. "I can't imagine that tough businessman softening for anyone. How soon?"

Piers shrugged. "Within a few days it looks like. Going to New York for the signing?"

"That's where his corporate offices are. I decided that when we began this I'd go there. Now, I'm not so sure."

"I might join you if you go. How about your wife?"

"Sara will be thrilled to hear the negotiations are progressing so well. She originally came to join her parents while they were here. I suspect she'll wish to continue that vacation when we separate. Has there been any further repercussions due to her actions?"

"All's quiet on the Garh and Hamin front. I think they are beginning to cave on their stance. It wouldn't look good, challenging the new wife of the negotiator, now would it?"

"And when we separate?" Kharun leaned back in his chair and studied his adviser. "What will be the repercussions then?"

"Ah, good question. Perhaps they will surge back stronger than ever in their anti-progress stance. Who can say at this point?"

Kharun rose and walked to the window. He didn't notice the beautiful blossoms in full bloom. Nor the glimpse of the sea beyond. He saw instead Sara's laughing face when she was happy, the sparkle in her silvery eyes when she was angry, and the graceful feminine way she had of walking or swimming or riding.

"Something wrong?" Piers asked, watching Kharun curiously.

"What would be the ramifications of a divorce instead of an annulment?" Kharun asked without turning.

The silence stretched out behind him.

Finally he turned to meet Piers's puzzled gaze.

"I don't understand." He blinked, slapped the side of his forehead with the heel of his hand. "Oh, damn, I do understand. Kharun, you and she didn't—"

"It is a hypothetical question," Kharun said firmly. At least at this point. But the desire he felt around Sara seemed to escalate each time he saw her. And he knew she was aware of the sparks that seemed to fly between them.

Yesterday at the stables, for a moment, he'd thought she'd start something. She'd looked at him intently, then color had risen in her cheeks. She'd been distant ever since. What had she been thinking?

Piers cleared his throat. "Actually, it might be better to divorce, than have an annulment. More believable, if you know what I mean."

"Elaborate."

"Let's face it, Kharun, no one in their right mind is going to think you and she didn't do anything—unless the marriage was a sham. It's one thing to fool your ministers—something else to let them know they've been fooled."

"Ah, so now you think it expedient to get a divorce rather than an annulment?"

"Can I have a few days to think over the situation?" Piers asked warily.

"Take as long as you like. It is hypothetical."

"But for how long, I wonder," his friend asked.

Sara appeared in the doorway, stopping suddenly when she saw Piers.

"Oh, excuse me, I didn't know you had company."

"Come in, Sara. You remember Piers."

"The best man. Of course. How are you?" She smiled warily, but remained at the doorway.

"Was there something you wanted?" Kharun asked politely.

"I wanted to phone my mother. She'll wonder why I haven't contacted her at all. I mean, I did come here to visit them, then disappeared. The next thing she knew, she was attending my wedding."

"She knows you are here and safe," Kharun said.

"So I can't call her?"

"Of course you can." He gestured to the phone.

Piers started to rise, but Kharun shook his head.

He turned to Kharun. "Is it wise, letting her phone?"

"Is it wise to raise suspicions of her parents by not allowing her contact?"

She remained in the doorway, watching the interchange. "I can wait until later, when you've finished your business," she said, turning to leave.

"This gets more complicated by the moment," Piers said.

"Actually, it would probably be all right to let her phone whenever she wishes. Sara gave me her word she'd abide by the terms of our agreement. I trust her to do just that."

Piers did blink at that comment. "You, trust a woman?"

"Within limits."

"That's a first. I thought after Andrea du Polline you'd sworn never to trust a woman again."

"This situation is different. Sara has concerns for her father's reputation, as well."

"As well as her own desire to stay out of one of our jails," Piers muttered sarcastically.

"That can be a strong motivating factor," Kharun agreed. "What did Kinsale concede on?"

Piers opened the folder he'd brought and looked at his friend. "I trust you know what you're doing about your marriage. And about the leases. Tell me what you think about this new counteroffer?" He indicated the paragraph of the report.

Kharun knew Piers was surprised by his comment. Hadn't he said often enough in the past he didn't trust women? They all appeared to be after one thing—his money. From his younger days in Eton, to his college days, and even the beginnings of his career, he'd been sought out by beautiful women who professed an interest in him alone—but had an eye on his inheritance.

Twice he'd come close to asking a woman to marry him, only to discover before he could ask the question that they were more interested in his wealth than their relationship. More interested in being seen in all the right places than in quiet dinners away from the "in" crowd.

How ironic, now he had married—and to a woman who didn't even *profess* to care for him. But by the same token, neither did she seem especially interested in his wealth or indulging in hectic nightlife.

Sara wandered around the patio feeling frustrated and bored. She needed to talk to her mother—though she'd have to reassure her she was deliriously happy being married and probably make vague plans for a dinner together at some point in the not-too-distant future.

Her mother was big on family. She'd adopt Kharun into their extended family immediately. Plopping down on a chaise longue, Sara moodily contemplated Kharun and her mother. How would he take to the informal family gatherings? Was he too steeped in tradition to fit in easily with her parents' casual private life? What did it matter? Theirs was a temporary alliance. They could stall any family overtures until time to separate.

For some reason, the thought didn't make her happy.

"Bonjour, Sara." Kharun's mother stood in the doorway and smiled at her.

Sara scrambled to her feet, surprised to see Angelique. Did Kharun know his mother was here?

"Good morning. I didn't know you were coming. Would you like to sit here, or is it too warm? Perhaps you'd rather go inside."

"Here, of course," Angelique said as she strolled onto the terrace. "The roses are lovely this year. But Matassin is a master gardener and has a special affinity for roses." She sat on the chair beside Sara's and indicated Sara should resume her own seat.

"I understand Kharun is back at work. So tiresome. But there is a lot to do. I do hope it won't be long before he can delegate enough to allow time off. If he ever does. His father loved his work. Runs in the family, I guess. I understand he's planning to go to New York to celebrate when the oil leases are signed. Maybe you and he can squeeze out a few extra days for a honeymoon then. You could show him your home—though I'm sure he's already seen it.''

Sara smiled politely, noncommittally. It was the first she'd heard about a possible trip back to the States. That could simplify things when they separated. She'd have to speak to Kharun about the trip.

''I came on the off chance he was back at work. I know my son, you see.''

''Piers was here first thing this morning to see him.''

''Then perhaps while they attend to business you would like to have lunch with me and Jasmine. Then you and I could stop in a few boutiques afterward, to look for a dress for Friday. Unless you already have a gown you planned to wear.''

''Friday?'' Sara asked.

''The reception at the British embassy. Surely Kharun plans to attend. I'm sure he wouldn't risk slighting everyone by not attending.''

''Friday night?'' Drat, she hated formal receptions. Especially any in which she was sure to be the center of attention. And as the new bride of Kharun bak Samin, she knew she'd be at the top of the list of people to stare at and gossip about.

''I wasn't sure if you brought an appropriate dress, but I'd be happy to introduce you to the delights of several boutiques in Staboul which can provide the most fabulous gowns on short notice.''

Sara wondered if one of them was the place Jasmine had found her wedding gown only an hour before the wedding.

"That would be lovely. I don't have anything suitable for an embassy reception. I'd love to come to lunch." Anything would be preferable to her almost enforced stay at the villa.

Angelique knew nothing of the truth. Jasmine knew, and didn't trust her. It should prove to be an interesting lunch.

Aminna appeared in the doorway, Sara's camera in hand.

"I found this in the kitchen when I returned this morning." Aminna held it out.

"My camera." Sara rose and crossed to the doorway to take it. "I left it there yesterday when I fixed lunch." Automatically, Sara checked the camera indicator.

"There's film in it!"

Aminna nodded gravely. "I saw it was empty and replaced the film. Do you wish to have lunch in the dining room, or on the terrace?"

"I'm taking my new daughter-in-law out to lunch, Aminna. Please inform Kharun."

Aminna nodded gravely and left.

"What a complicated camera. I didn't know you were a photographer. How exciting. What do you like to shoot?" Angelique asked.

Pictures of your summer home without your knowledge, popped into Sara's mind.

"Um, actually I'm still developing my style. I like working to get the right framing, contrast the light and shadows. Things like that."

"What do you photograph? People? Scenes? Closeups of plants?"

"Horses, odd houses, old ruins." She smiled. "Sometimes people. Whatever I find interesting." She'd been taking photographs of her family and friends, of exotic locations and quiet homey places for years. The results had been gratifying. She'd been focused on her aborted plan to get pictures of the Samin's summer place, hoping for unusual angles to make the shots distinctive. Maybe today she could get snapshots of Staboul to take home when she left.

And later, she'd photograph the villa. Surely no one could find fault with her taking photos of her own home, however temporary.

Aminna came quietly onto the terrace, a laden tray of tea and small cakes in her hands. She efficiently set the table, placed the food in the center and returned to the house, never saying a word.

"I would like to photograph her," Sara said musingly. "Her face has such character." She faced Angelique as she poured their tea. "And I'd love to photograph your son riding Satin Magic."

"Do so. If it turns out, I would love to have a copy. He is a fine-looking man, isn't he?" She looked at Sara from beneath her lashes.

The true reason a mother had come—to find out more about her son's new wife. Sara smiled politely, wondering how his mother would feel if she knew Sara's true feelings.

Suddenly, she realized she wasn't even sure of her true feelings. Granted, she felt confined to the house since he'd rescued her from the jail. Understandable, though frustrating. She was counting the days until she would be free.

Yet she was strangely intrigued by the man. Fascinated by the range of sensations that danced through her when in his presence. She liked sparring with him, liked hearing him discuss the matters of change he wanted for his country.

She was completely captivated by his kisses. She warmed at the memory. The last time they'd had someone not privy to their secret come to visit, he'd kissed her. Would he kiss her in his mother's presence?

Her heart rate sped up a notch.

She'd soon find out. Kharun stepped out onto the terrace.

CHAPTER SIX

"MA MÈRE, Aminna told me you were here. I wasn't expecting you." Kharun glanced at Sara as he crossed the terrace to kiss his mother on both cheeks.

"I didn't mean to interrupt you, *chéri.* Aminna told me you were hard at work. I thought Sara might have enticed you away from your duties for a little longer. First you take no honeymoon, now you neglect her. For shame." The twinkle in her eyes belied her words.

"Things needed to be done. Sara understands."

"Always things need to be done. Your new wife is a saint if she allows it. Such virtue deserves a reward. I'm taking Sara to lunch with me and Jasmine. Unless, of course, you have plans yourself."

"Piers is here. We are working."

"Times have changed from when I was young," she said mockingly, with a conspiratorial look at Sara.

"How so?"

"Your father and I made sure our priorities included a long honeymoon."

"It never ended."

Her face saddened. "Not until his death. Cherish the moments you have, *chéri,* they seem so fleeting in retrospect."

She rose and patted him on the cheek. "I will speak with Aminna for a moment, then Sara and I will leave.

We're going shopping after lunch. Bring your camera, Sara, you can start with Jasmine and me.''

He waited until she was out of hearing, then turned to Sara, apparently noticing the camera for the first time.

''Aminna brought me the camera. She found it in the kitchen,'' Sara said, holding it in front of her, almost like a shield. ''You mother suggested the photographs.''

''Take the pictures she wants, then. But I'll have the film developed,'' he said with a warning in his tone. ''And none are to go to your newspaper!''

Sara stiffened. She knew he didn't truly trust her, due to her own actions, but it still rankled. ''I have no intention of sending any to the paper!''

''Jasmine knows the true story about our marriage, but my mother doesn't. Keep it that way,'' he admonished.

''Did you come out here just to tell me that? Of course I can remember that order from one day to the next. No one is to know. If I can't tell my mother, I surely won't be telling yours!''

She hurried into the house to change from the modest white pants she'd donned that morning into something more suitable to lunch with her new in-laws.

When she entered the large foyer several minutes later, Piers and Angelique were talking. Kharun leaned casually against the priceless Louis XV table watching them. He looked at Sara when she joined them. She wondered for a moment if the gleam in his eyes meant more than he still didn't trust her.

''Have a good afternoon,'' he said, deliberately crossing to her. He stood so close she could almost share his breath—if she hadn't been holding hers.

"I wish I were going with you," he said. Only she understood the full truth of the comment. He was wary about letting her out of his sight. Yet his comment undoubtedly sounded totally different to his mother, she was sure. Angelique thought Kharun longed to spend the day with his new bride. If she only knew!

"I'll be back before dinner—nothing will happen." It was the best she could do to offer reassurance.

His lips brushed against hers and he straightened and turned.

It wasn't enough. Sara gripped the straps of her purse tightly. She wanted more!

Yet the brief kiss was more than she could have expected.

Pasting a bright smile on her face she faced Angelique. "Let's do lunch!"

When the women had left, Piers looked at Kharun. "Is that wise?"

"Probably not. But it caused no comment. If I had kept Sara isolated from my mother, she would wonder why, and begin to question me, and speculate to all and sundry. I dare not risk any suspicion."

"I understand, but what's to stop Sara from running off the first moment Angelique turns her back?"

Kharun paused a moment, deep in thought. "Sara said she would stay, I believe her."

"She could be a spy. At best she's a sensationalist hack journalist searching for fodder for that rag she works for."

"But she *is* Samuel Kinsale's daughter. His ethics

have never been questioned. I'm betting she's enough like her father that she won't disappear.''

''I hope you're right,'' Piers said, heading back toward the office.

''Me, too,'' Kharun said softly. He wasn't sure where the feeling of total trust had come from. His experience with women outside his family had done nothing to foster such a trust. But there was something about Sara—

He shook his head and followed his friend back to work. He hoped he wasn't letting his desire for the woman cloud his judgment.

When Angelique's chauffeur dropped Sara back at the villa later that afternoon, Sara held the half dozen bags of purchases balanced in her arms. She rang the bell and wondered if she should have asked for a key.

One of the maids opened the door, smiling shyly when she recognized Sara. She said something in Arabic, which of course Sara didn't understand. Replying in French, she could tell the young woman didn't speak that language. It was frustrating not being able to communicate. But the nods and smiles seemed sufficient.

Sara headed for her room. The afternoon had been unexpectedly fun. Jasmine never let up her cautious air, which thankfully Angelique didn't appear to notice. Sara answered all their questions, dared to ask a couple of her own, and tried to pretend everything was normal for a newly wed woman getting to know her new in-laws.

But always in the background hovered the specter of Kharun and the reality of the true situation.

"Shopping, a woman's delight," Kharun said behind her.

Sara spun around, the packages flying every which way.

"I didn't hear you!" she accused. How did he move so soundlessly?

"My apologies." He leaned over and picked up two of the bags.

Sara reached for the others, and continued on to her room feeling a little snappy, with butterflies dancing in her stomach. What was wrong with her? Too much chocolate mousse for dessert at lunch?

Her skin seemed to tingle at his closeness. She wished she'd checked her hair, made sure her lipstick was fresh. Anticipation hummed through her veins.

He followed her into the bedroom as if he had every right. Which, she thought wryly, he did.

"I bought some things," she said needlessly, dumping her bags on the bed. Kharun placed the two he carried and looked at her, his dark eyes disturbing. She fidgeted beneath his gaze.

"What did you buy?" he asked politely.

"A dress for the reception at the British embassy. Your mother said we would be going."

He nodded his head once.

"When were you planning on telling me?" she asked. "Ten minutes before we were about to leave? Listen to me, Kharun, arranging my life without telling me is not something which I'll put up with." She waved her hands. "The first I knew about our wedding was when Jasmine showed up with the dress. The first I knew about this reception was when your mother told me. What else is going on that I need to know that you haven't told me?''

He shrugged. ''I will have to check my calendar. Would you like to go over it with me?'' he asked politely, amusement dancing in his eyes.

She flushed at the sardonic glint in his eyes.

''Of course not, just let me know ahead of time if there is an event you expect me to attend. And I will let you know, as well.''

He quirked an eyebrow. ''An event you and I would attend that you arranged?''

''My mother will certainly wish to have us over for dinner soon. The few moments we had to talk after our hasty wedding certainly weren't enough to satisfy her curiosity. Nor could we talk while I packed with you hovering around like a vulture.''

''Vulture? Somehow I had hoped for a more romantic turn of phrase. I thought I played the part of doting bridegroom perfectly.''

''I'm sure you'd have received rave reviews if anyone had known. But my mother's big on family. She'll love welcoming you into ours, the sooner the better for her.''

Sara bit her lower lip. ''We'll have to stall her.''

''Why is that?''

''There's no point in her getting used to you when the marriage will be over soon.''

''As you say. Let me see the gown.''

She thought about arguing, but about what? She knew this was solely a marriage of convenience—his convenience. Showing him the clothes effectively changed the subject. Sara was pleased with her selections and wondered what he'd think about them. She pushed aside two of the smaller bags, taking the larger one. Withdrawing the dress, wrapped in layers and layers of tissue paper, she shook it free.

Almost a midnight-blue, shot through with silver threads, it was the loveliest dress she'd ever seen. And it fit like a dream.

She held it up, and looked at him.

His expression gave nothing away.

"Try it on," he invited.

"Now?"

"It's hard to see how it will look on you when merely held up in front." He walked to the sitting area and sat as if he was settled for the rest of the afternoon.

"I guess I could."

Five minutes later Sara emerged from the bathroom dressed in the new gown.

The high jeweled halter neckline gave a false impression of modesty belied by the fitted bodice and the long slinky skirt that sported a slit up one side to mid-thigh. The back was virtually nonexistent until her waist. Sara felt alluring and mysterious wearing it.

She should have found the shoes first, however. Walking barefoot missed the look.

Or maybe not, if the heightened awareness of Kharun's interest was a gauge. He rose and walked to meet her halfway across the room.

"You look exquisite," he said slowly, his gaze running along the length of her body. Heat built as he continued to study her. "Turn around."

Slowly she turned around completely, hearing the hiss as he drew in a sharp breath when he saw her bare back.

"Won't you be cold in that?" he asked, his voice rough.

Sara shook her head. If she didn't bank the fires his look caused, she'd burn up.

"I think I'll be fine," she said, pleased to hear her own voice sounded normal. "Your mother helped pick it out."

"My mother is a Frenchwoman, of course she'd pick out something wildly sexy."

"Wildly sexy? Cool!"

He reached out to draw a warm finger down her bare arm. "The men will be envious of my good fortune. The women will be jealous of your beauty," he said slowly.

Her heart almost flipped over. No one had ever said anything so wonderful to her before.

Mesmerized by the heat in his eyes, Sara stared back at him, licking suddenly dry lips.

Kharun caught the movement and fastened his attention on her mouth.

Before she could say anything, he drew her into his arms and kissed her.

There was no audience, was her last coherent thought before dazzling sensation took over.

His mouth sparked a cascade of shimmering enchantment. Sara stepped closer, as if seeking more. She parted her lips and instantly felt Kharun deepen the kiss. His warm hands on her bare back sent tingling waves of excitement coursing through her. His tongue dancing with hers caused the desire that simmered to explode.

She yearned for more. She couldn't get enough of him. She wanted to taste him everywhere, touch him everywhere. Her hands threaded through his thick hair, relishing the texture and heat. She moved them to trace the muscles of his shoulders, back to his head. When he slowly spun them around, she felt as if the world tilted. She clung, holding on to the one steadfast reality in a fantasy illusion.

Slowly they moved until she felt the world fall away. Only it was the two of them, falling onto the bed, amid the bags, tissue paper and pillows.

He held her tightly, cushioning their soft fall, moving his mouth from hers to her cheek, tracing her jaw, running his tongue lightly against her throat, kissing that frantically beating pulse point.

Sara lay half across him, feeling the rugged strength of his chest beneath her. Savoring the feel of his hands against her skin, touching her, caressing her.

The fresh breeze blowing across the garden from the sea brought with it the scent of flowers and the salt air but no cooling relief for the building heat. She was spellbound by the sensations that clamored for dominance—desire, shivering enchantment, sensuous languor.

When Kharun ran his hand down her side, slipping beneath the bodice of the gown to graze her breast, Sara caught her breath. For an instant sanity reasserted itself.

She pushed back, gazing down at him. Slowly he opened his eyes and gazed back.

Scrambling off the bed, Sara backed away. The breeze suddenly felt cold. The dress offered so little protection.

''What is going on?'' she asked. The forceful demand

she had hoped to make fell flat. It came out almost a whisper.

Kharun rose lithely and took a step toward her. Sara backed away, clinging almost desperately to the shred of common sense that told her things were getting out of hand. One part of her wanted to throw herself back into his embrace. Another part questioned her sanity.

"I kissed you, you kissed me back."

"That went far beyond a mere kiss!"

"And that upsets you?"

"Of course it does. What's going on? We agreed to a farce of a marriage to make sure we avoided a scandal. But we agreed it would be strictly platonic."

"I'm afraid I don't remember such an agreement."

She blinked. They had said—what exactly? "I remember in the car—"

He waited, as a panther might wait before leaping on his prey, silently, without moving, but aware of everything. Sara took a nervous step backward.

Her eyes widened as she remembered. They'd been discussing the right to share a bed. She'd said he had to stay out of hers and she'd stay out of his. But now that she recalled the conversation, he had never agreed.

"The dress was a mistake," she said.

"Why? It looks lovely on you."

"It obviously gave the wrong message."

Kharun laughed and shook his head, heading for the door. "Sara, the sight of you in that dress did not inflame passion." He paused at the door and looked back at her. "Just looking at you does that. Whether in jeans or bedraggled khakis. I came to see if you wished to ride again this afternoon?''

She blinked, trying to regain her balance. Had he just said he felt desire for her just by looking at her? Then he asked about riding?

''Ride?''

''Horses?''

The sardonic glint was back. He probably thought her mind had been fried by their kiss.

He wasn't far off the mark.

''Yes, I'd love to go riding. I'll change now and meet you at the stables.''

Kharun waited impatiently in the foyer for Sara to change. He had not trusted himself to stay in her room while she slipped out of that sexy gown and donned jeans.

He hadn't wanted to stop when she'd called a halt. He wanted her. And it had been a long time since he had felt such a strong sense of wanting for a woman.

Brief flings in distant capitals had been the norm over the last few years after his blazing mistake with Andrea du Polline. He'd made a fool of himself over her. She'd made a fool of herself over his money.

And since his father had died, he had not had the time, nor inclination, to seek out female companionship.

But Sara was different. Was that part of the spark that drove him crazy? He was sure she felt something around him. He was too savvy not to recognize the signs. Their kiss had been all he'd hoped. But she'd stopped long before he was ready.

He almost laughed. She thought it was the dress. Did she really not have a clue? Or was she playing a more devious game?

''I'm ready.'' Sara joined him, dressed in jeans, a long-sleeved cotton top and her shoes. He'd have to see about her getting some riding boots. Especially if they went to the desert. Would Sara like riding across the dunes, chasing the stars at night?

They could escape away from everything—until they were alone in the universe. He'd dismount and help her from the saddle, letting her body slide down his, a temptation he knew he couldn't resist. Spreading a blanket on the sands still warm from the day's sun, he'd lay her down and strip her bare—until her soft, feminine skin was bathed in starlight. Then he'd make love to her until dawn.

''Kharun, are we going?''

He looked at her. Yes, one night he'd take her to the desert and make love to her.

''After you.'' He opened the door and waited.

She preceded him and turned toward the walkway that led to the stables. He watched her walk, tall and proud. Her hips swayed gently in the tight jeans.

He felt his own pants tighten against him. But he couldn't look away. He thought about what Piers had said—better a divorce than an annulment—at least the ministers might be fooled by such a decision. An annulment would be a slap in the face.

And after everyone had met her, no one would believe an annulment anyway.

Theirs was a temporary alliance, true. But Kharun

knew something bound them tightly for however long she stayed. He would make Sara his wife in truth as well as on paper.

When they reached the stables, he reached out and took an arm, halting her.

"What?"

"Just so you know, it wasn't the dress."

He leaned over to kiss her again, pleased to note the instant response on her part.

The horses were already saddled. Kharun helped Sara to mount, then swung up onto his own horse. He led the way to the beach, wishing again he was on the desert. The confines of the city and demands of his new position grated. He needed to feel the space and freedom of the desert. Soon, he'd schedule a week and forget Staboul and his uncle's interfering ministers and show Sara the other delights of his country.

Once he reached the beach, he gave Satin Magic his head. He was not surprised to find Sara racing neck and neck beside him in only seconds. Alia was a match for Satin. He urged his horse to greater speed, relishing the sense of freedom, the exhilaration riding Satin always brought.

They thundered down the beach, splashing in the shallows, scattering rainbows of colors behind them, tossing up the sand in a wake they could track. Purely for his own pleasure, Kharun kept up the fast pace, but he also was attuned to Sara. If it became too much, he'd stop.

But she was a woman to rise to challenges. She did her best to coax a faster gait from Alia, never giving up.

The sun sparkled on the water, the air was scented

with the fragrance of a thousand flowers. Blood pulsed in his veins. It was a great day in which to be alive, made all the more so with Sara's presence.

The thought caught him by surprise.

Seeing the signs of civilization ahead, he slowed Satin. Alia raced past, then slowed and turned. Sara halted, breathing hard, as she waited for Kharun to reach her. Her face was ablaze with happiness.

"That was wonderful!" she said, then burst into laughter. "What a fantasy—racing a sheikh along the sea. Splashing in the water. I'm wet to my knees."

He felt a chill. Was that all the afternoon meant—a fantasy with a title, instead of the real thing with a man who desired her? Was she like the others, after all, caught up in the trappings of wealth and titles?

Even after the hard run, Alia danced in place, anxious to continue.

"What's wrong?" Sara asked, controlling her mount, and holding her still.

"Not a thing. You ride well."

"It's not hard on a sweetie like Alia. She seems ready to continue."

"They have a lot of stamina. I breed them for endurance."

"Do you ever take them out in the desert?"

How had her mind aligned itself with his? Was it fate?

"Sometimes."

"I'd love to try that, if we get a chance. I imagine it's even more wonderful—riding forever in the empty desert. No sign of civilization for miles and miles. There are places like that in the States and I love being there. Maybe I should have been a hermit in another life.''

He edged his horse closer, facing Sara, until their knees almost touched.

She was still breathing fast, her breasts rising and falling rapidly. Her gaze caught his, drifted to his mouth. Did she want another kiss? Was she as caught up in the sensual awareness as he?

Her lids drooped and she looked away, color staining her cheeks.

Kharun felt a wave of satisfaction sweep through. She couldn't hide her own awareness. Now it was only a matter of time before he had her in his bed.

Knowing that gave him the will to be more patient. He would not rush her.

But soon.

Sara started her horse back toward the villa. Kharun turned and eased Satin Magic into step with Alia. The horses tossed their heads, but he and Sara kept them to a walk.

''What else was in the packages you brought home?'' he asked.

''Another dress, and a couple of pairs of shoes. Your mother is a power shopper. She was telling us at lunch how she splurges every now and then and goes to Paris.''

''For her, that is the only place really worth shopping.''

''Yet she loves this country, that much is evident in her conversation.'' Sara cast a sidelong glance. ''And she is very pro you.''

"And you find that surprising? Aren't most mothers for their children?"

"Does she know the real you?"

"Who is the real me?"

"A man who manipulates events to his own purposes."

Kharun suspected where the conversation was headed. Could he defuse it?

"Did you take pictures?"

"I got some great ones. Jasmine was quite annoyed with me by the end of the afternoon. Every time I'd see something new, I'd ask Yasaf, your mother's chauffeur, to stop. Your mother, on the other hand, seemed happy to have me photograph anything that took my fancy— from the lovely inlays lining the outside of a mosque, to the faces of children in the poorer section of town."

"You went to the Sadinn area of town?"

"I think that's what it was called. Angelique gave me a complete tour before we stopped at the first boutique."

Why had his mother done so? She didn't know the full circumstances of his marriage, but even if it had been a true love match, wouldn't she shelter her new daughter-in-law from the rougher sections of town until Sara became more accustomed to their country?

"Your mother offered to have the film developed. I told her you wanted to do so, but she insisted she didn't want to wait to see what I'd done. I'm sure you can intercept them when she brings them over to make sure I'm not photographing top secret places in my role as spy."

CHAPTER SEVEN

KHARUN was going to drive her crazy, Sara just knew it. It wasn't enough he suspected her of being a spy, now he was on some campaign to seduce her. Did he think she would then confess to some nefarious plot?

She paused with mascara wand in hand and peered into the mirror. She had ten more minutes before they were due to depart for the British embassy reception.

She glanced over to the bed and looked at the dress. Would she ever be able to wear it without remembering Kharun's kisses and caresses the afternoon she modeled it for him?

She doubted it. She looked back to the mirror and touched her lashes with the mascara. She was nervous about the evening. She disliked large gatherings, how would she handle being the mysterious new bride of Sheikh Kharun bak Samin? She was sure to be the cynosure of all eyes.

"It's just pretend," she murmured, knowing no one else there would think so.

Her hair brushed, her makeup on—she could put it off no longer. She donned the dress. Immediately she was enveloped in the sensuous feelings she had experienced when she'd modeled it for Kharun. The silky material hugged her body like a second skin. The breeze from the veranda caressed her bare back. Slipping on the high heels, she walked to the full-length mirror. The dress

116

made her eyes look silvery. Nervousness gave color to her cheeks. She rubbed her stomach, trying to quell the butterflies. But she couldn't help wondering how Kharun would react when he saw her again in the sexiest dress she'd ever owned.

No time like the present to find out.

She grabbed a small, jeweled purse and headed out, head held high.

Kharun was waiting for her. His tux was elegantly tailored, fashioned for his wide shoulders, long legs. The ruffled shirt might have looked effeminate on other men, but on him it accentuated his rugged masculinity. He looked as daring as a pirate—or a desert raider.

She walked up to him, holding his gaze with her own. Butterflies danced in her stomach and she had trouble breathing, but she wouldn't let him know. Tilting her chin slightly, she stopped right next to him—much closer than she needed to be. Two could play this sensuous game. She almost touched the arm of his jacket, but settled for looking at him from beneath her lashes and smiling.

"You look lovely," he said. Taking her hand in his, he raised it to his lips. Brushing the back with his lips, he turned it slightly until he could brush the sensitive inner skin of her wrist.

Sara felt a shock of desire flood through her. Almost yanking her hand free, she tried to hold her smile. "Is it time to leave?"

He inclined his head, the amusement in his eyes disturbing her. So much for trying to maintain a sophisticated veneer. She turned to head for the door and heard him catch his breath. The sound gave her a smidgeon of satisfaction—he was still affected by the dress, or lack of its back. Good. She hated to be the only one lost in a fog.

The limousine swiftly transported them to the British embassy. The old building was made of stone, with tall columns holding a wide portico in front. Lights shone from all the many ground-floor windows. As they left the limousine, they could hear the murmur of voices and soft background music wafting out on the warm evening air.

Without time to even think, Sara was whisked up the stairs and into the huge reception hall. The short receiving line was solely comprised of the ambassador and his wife and another high-ranking official from England.

Show time, Sara thought. She slipped her hand onto Kharun's arm. He bent his arm and held her hand close to his body. Head held high, she stepped out and the evening began.

An hour later Sara thought her face would crack from smiling so much. She had met everyone in the room, she was certain, and answered so many questions about how she and Kharun met that she wished she'd printed up cards to hand out.

Kharun stayed by her side, giving her snippets of information about the people she met before he exchanged greetings with them. He seemed to know everyone, she thought, wondering how much longer the evening would last. She longed for the privacy of her room.

To add to the strain, she made every effort to play the part of adoring bride. Why had she ever thought she wanted a career in acting? It was hard to remember to glance up to Kharun with what she hoped was love in her gaze from time to time. Primarily because she was so busy trying to focus on breathing. His touch seemed to short-circuit her normal functions. His hand rested on her bare back at one point and she almost forgot the question he asked her. When he laced his fingers through hers later in the evening, her breath caught again. At the rate she was going, she would be a basket case by the end of the reception.

"Ah, Your Excellency, I have not yet had the opportunity to meet your charming bride."

Sara turned at the sound of the voice. She took an instant dislike to the man standing beside them. He was not tall, Sara could look him in the eye. His dark gaze narrowed and his voice oozed oily *bonhomie*, which did not cover his insincerity. She wondered if he thought it did.

"Garh Sonharh, my wife Sara. Darling, Garh is one of my uncle's most trusted new ministers." Kharun's voice was neutral, void of any intonation that would give Sara a hint of how he felt about the man. And that in itself was a clue.

The name was familiar—she suddenly remembered. It was after talking with this man that Kharun had come up with the outlandish scheme to marry instead of just an engagement.

"How do you do, sir?" she said sweetly, smiling as vapidly as she could. Maybe the acting lessons would come in handy, after all. "I'm so delighted to meet you."

Kharun's hand tightened on hers. She resisted looking at him, knowing she might burst into laughter. Then the seriousness of the matter reasserted itself. This man could be considered an enemy of her husband—and of her father. If he suspected they weren't truly married he could precipitate that international incident she was trying to avoid.

"Did you get those photographs you wanted for your husband?" Garh asked.

"Photographs? Oh, of the summer villa? Unfortunately there was a misunderstanding about that." Sara looked up at Kharun, hoping her expression would be taken as adoring. "We got it cleared up, though, didn't we, darling?"

Suddenly she looked straight at Garh. "But how did you hear about that?"

Garh inclined his head slightly. "Rumors, only, madam."

"There you are, I've been looking all over for you," Jasmine said. She wore a burgundy gown and looked stunning.

"Minister Sonharh," she included him in her greeting, then smiled at Sara. "Come and meet some friends of mine. Yasife is dying to meet an American. I told her all about you and Kharun's wildly romantic courtship."

"Do not end up gossiping with the women all night long," Kharun said, kissing the back of Sara's hand before releasing his hold. He turned to Garh as the two women left.

"Thanks," Sara said softly, once out of earshot.

Jasmine laughed. "Garh's bite is worse than his bark and that's formidable. He is against everything Kharun wants to do—from the oil deal to improving the infrastructure, to enticing tourists to boost our economy. I don't know why Kharun doesn't prevail upon our uncle to get rid of him," Jasmine said with a frown.

"Have you asked him?"

"He says it's easier to keep an eye on him at the ministerial level than to constantly wonder what the man might be doing behind his back. Come, here's Yasife."

"So, how did your first reception in Kamtansin go?" Kharun asked as they settled in the limousine after bidding their hosts farewell two hours later.

"Better than I expected," Sara admitted. She kicked off her shoes and wiggled her toes. Frowning, she then wrinkled up her face.

"Is something wrong?"

"I thought I'd try to relax my facial muscles. I hope you don't expect a smile out of me for two days. It'll be that long before my cheeks stop aching."

He laughed softly. The sound was like mulled wine on a cold winter's day. It seeped through Sara, warm and intoxicating.

"I hope you don't expect me to remember the names of the four million people I met tonight," she said brightly to cover her reactions.

"It was only a few dozen, and no, for the most part, you'll remember them after seeing them again and again at various functions. There are a few who are personal friends, do remember them, please."

"Who?" She rested her head against the cushions and closed her eyes, listening to Kharun talk. She could listen to his voice from now until forever.

She felt a brush against her cheek. Slowly she opened her eyes. Kharun was leaning over her.

"We're home."

Sara blinked, awareness gradually returning. Awareness of Kharun growing.

"Did I fall asleep?"

"Just as I was telling you about some friends. I'll have to make sure I don't bore you next time."

"Oh, no, not that!" She sat up, pressing against his shoulder. "I'm sorry. I was just so tired from the strain of the reception—and meeting Garh Sonharh. Jasmine told me about him. He's the real reason we got married, isn't he? He doesn't suspect anything, does he? Jasmine said he was a real thorn in your side."

"I can handle Garh. Come, you can be in bed in only a couple of minutes."

She followed him into the villa and turned to head for her room when he stopped her.

"Your acting was more than adequate for our deception. Thank you for tonight." He leaned closer and kissed her.

Still half-asleep, still remembering the intoxicating effect of his voice in the darkness of the car, Sara stepped into his embrace and his kiss.

The lassitude from her brief nap vanished. Blood began to pound through her veins as his mouth caressed hers, as his lips moved persuasively to coax hers into a response. When she parted her lips, his tongue teased her. She returned the favor, relishing the wild freedom she felt when in Kharun's arms.

His hands were warm on her bare back, sending tendrils of pure pleasure through her. She encircled his neck with her arms and tried to get even closer. She could feel the hard length of him against her and savored the differences between them.

She felt as if she were floating.

He ended the kiss, resting his forehead on hers and gazing deep into her eyes when she reluctantly opened them. The fiery passion he kept under strict control was visible in his eyes. The desire he couldn't completely hide sent a shiver of anticipation and reckless abandonment through her. What would it be like to make love with Kharun?

"You had better go to bed now, if you wish to sleep alone," his voice said roughly.

Sara hesitated a split second. One part of her didn't want to go to bed alone, but the other part knew it would be a mistake not to. This was a temporary, short-term, marriage-in-name-only, not the prelude to a lifelong commitment.

She nodded, pulled her arms from around his neck and turned, walking swiftly to her room.

"Damn!" he said softly as the door closed behind her. Angrily, he ran the fingers of one hand through his hair, and back to his neck, easing some of the tension. Since when had he become a blasted Boy Scout? He wasn't known for his altruism. He was ruthless in his pursuit of a business deal, or in dealing with mistakes at work.

If he'd kept his mouth on hers, they would be in bed together at this very moment. Instead, he was left in the hallway, staring at a blank door as if he hoped for X-ray vision to see through to Sara's room.

She was probably sliding out of that dress now. It clung to her like a second skin, showing off every delectable curve and valley. He wanted to be the one to slip it from her shoulders, to watch it puddle at her feet on the floor, then raise his gaze to see her wearing nothing at all.

Turning before he did something rash, Kharun strode to his own bedroom. What had possessed him to put her in the room the farthest from his own? What if she needed something in the night?

Like what? his consciousness jeered. Someone to tuck her into bed? Someone to soothe away any nightmares?

Someone to kiss her to sleep?

The truth was he wasn't used to denying himself anything. All evening he'd watched for a sign from Sara that she wasn't immune to the sparks that seemed to fill the room whenever the two of them were together.

Just a hint, and he would not have sent her to bed alone.

But either she was a terrific actress, or she didn't have a clue. Or maybe she didn't feel the attraction he felt, didn't find anything intriguing about him, like he did with her. Perhaps she was counting the days until the oil deal was finalized and she could return to her parents.

For a moment, the thought of Sara returning to America, never returning to Kamtansin, was more than he cared to deal with. He'd better make the most of her stay. Once she was gone, he'd likely never see her again.

The next morning Kharun ate alone. He wondered if Sara was avoiding him, or just tired from last night and sleeping in. He almost went to check, but for the arrival of his mother.

"Good morning, Kharun," she said, smiling as he

rose to greet her. "I hope I'm not visiting too early, but I'm excited about a project I think you will love." Angelique looked around. "Where is Sara?"

"We went to the embassy reception last night, she's sleeping in this morning."

"No, I'm not. I just got a late start," Sara said from the doorway.

Kharun looked at her and schooled his features to hide his reaction. She looked lovely today—her blond hair like a nimbus around her face. Despite her claim to not smile for a week, she was smiling at his mother. For a moment he was jealous of that smile. Sara never smiled at him that way.

Foolishness! He greeted her formally and held a chair for his mother. Sara went to the far side of the table and sat down before he could reach her.

Aminna entered, carrying a tray of croissants, muffins, and various breads. She placed it in the center of the table, pausing to greet Kharun's mother.

Kharun waited until everyone had begun to eat before asking his mother why she'd come to visit so early.

"I thought it would be the best time to reach you both—before you began work for the day and Sara took off."

"Took off?" He looked at Sara.

She shrugged. "I'm not going anywhere."

"You will once you see what I've brought," Angelique said. She smiled at her son. "You will love this."

She rose and left the room, returning two minutes later with a handful of photographs.

With a dramatic gesture, she spread them on the table beside Kharun.

He glanced at the pictures and then at his mother. "And they are?"

"The photographs Sara took."

Sara rose and looked over Kharun's shoulder at the pictures.

"They're the ones I took the other day when Angelique drove me around Staboul." She smiled when she saw the little children crowding around a tourist. "That one came out well, it looks just like I imagined it."

Kharun studied each one in turn. There weren't many. He looked at his mother. She was brimming with excitement.

"Nice pictures," he said.

"Kharun—they're perfect for use as a tourist draw. What person seeing these wouldn't want to come to visit our country?"

"Tourist draw?" Sara repeated.

"It's one of Kharun's and Jasmine's special projects. They've been assigned unofficially to initiate a tourist bureau. We want more visitors to our country—to boost the economy, to share our lovely beaches with those who like to vacation at the sea, to show our historic buildings and offer another attraction for the world traveler. Kharun, don't you see? These are perfect. Sara could take more, and work on a brochure we could then send to the world! And think of the interest because Sara took them."

"I don't know what you mean," Kharun said slowly, but he suspected.

"Thanks to the clandestine manner of your marriage, you are making headlines in all the world's press. People read newspapers! There is a fascination with wealthy men, and an aura around those who don't normally seek publicity. Capitalize on it, as you always say!"

Sara looked at him in horror. "We're in the newspapers?"

He glanced over and almost smiled at her horrified expression. "We're news, why not. Isn't that what you said initially—once in the public eye privacy vanishes?"

He wanted to brush away the lines her frown caused, caress her cheek, excuse themselves from his mother and take her into another part of the house to kiss and caress and see if he could spark an answering desire in this golden girl.

Instead, he forced himself to look away and give serious consideration to the suggestion his mother made.

He picked up the pictures and studied each one in detail. Two he tossed aside, they were good but nothing special. But the rest he held captured his attention. Would they work toward promoting his country? The added money tourists would bring would help finance the improvements he and his father had tirelessly worked for. As would the oil deal he was trying to conclude.

"Would you be interested in taking more photographs, with that end in view?" he asked Sara.

She blinked and nodded, looking amazed. Once again he wanted to whisk her away where the two of them could be alone and undisturbed.

Sara took the photographs from Kharun, careful not to touch his fingers, he noticed. He watched as she studied each one in turn. Slowly her smile came out.

"I did pretty well, didn't I?" She looked up and he caught the slight catch in her breath. Satisfaction swept through. She wasn't as immune to the attraction between them as she'd been pretending. It wasn't one-sided! Wasn't that interesting?

"So you'll do more?" Angelique asked impatiently.

"I would be delighted, if you think any picture I take would be worth something," Sara said, stepping away as if she'd get burned if she stayed so close to him.

"Tourism has not been made a formal part of the government as of yet," he said slowly once they'd all resumed their seats and began eating again. "Jasmine and I have asked our uncle to make it a priority, but he moves slowly."

"He's a turtle when it comes to change," his mother said. "Oh, the arguments your father and he had!" She smiled mistily, remembering.

"A fresh perspective would be good, as well. If you'd let us know what appeals to you about visiting our country, we can capitalize on that."

Angelique laughed softly. "This will be wonderful. And give Sara something to do while you are working. This is supposed to be your honeymoon. But if you insist on working during the day, Sara needs something to occupy herself. And what better time than now, when everything is fresh and new to her. Once she's lived here for a few decades, it'll be as if she's always been here. At least that's how I feel."

Kharun looked at Sara, his eyes focusing on the color that sprang into her cheeks, the way she shyly looked at him. Only the two of them knew Sara wouldn't be here for decades. In fact, she may only remain another week or two, until the final papers were signed and the oil agreements firmly in place.

Sara glanced away and tried to take a deep breath. As long as she didn't look at Kharun or touch him, or think about him, she could do this. Surely the oil agreements would be signed soon and their pretense come to an end—hopefully before she made a complete idiot of herself.

But she couldn't stop the warm glow that filled her at his comments. Kharun liked her photographs. Angelique liked them. She stared at the photos again. They were good, even she could see it.

Was this finally something she could build upon? Make a career with photography? Expand on a hobby and make it into something broader than photojournalism? Maybe specialize in scenes for travel brochures?

Taking pictures would be fun, occupy her time and keep her from fantasizing about Kharun.

"I'm happy to take more photos. It's fun."

Aminna appeared in the doorway. She spoke to Kharun.

"It appears your mother is on the phone, wishing to speak with you, Sara," he said. "You may take it in the hallway if you wish, for privacy."

Aminna held out a portable phone to Sara when she reached the door. She smiled her thanks and continued walking, putting the phone to her ear.

"Mother?"

"Hi, sweetie, how are things going? When are you and Kharun coming to dinner with your father and me?

We will be returning home in a few days, surely you can spare enough time for one dinner.''

"You're going home?''

"As soon as the oil agreements are finalized and your father says that'll be soon. So we need to get together soon, or I'll have to fly halfway 'round the world to have dinner!''

"I'll check with Kharun and call you back.''

"Any night next week would work for us. And in the meantime, what about lunch—just you and me. I want to know more about you and Kharun. The wedding came as a complete surprise and we haven't had a chance to talk properly since.''

"Sure, Mom, let me check and call you back. I'd like to have lunch.'' Not. How would she keep the truth from her mother, who knew her so well. She'd just have to stall, or invite Angelique along so there could be no heart-to-heart.

"Oh, one other thing, do you know a Pete Steede?'' her mother asked.

Her editor at the newspaper. "Yes. He's my boss. How did you know his name?''

"He has called at least half a dozen times, insisting he talk with you. Maybe you better return the call to keep him from leaving any more messages. He's a bit pushy.''

Sara almost laughed. Pete was beyond pushy. How like her mother to be so diplomatic.

"I'll call him right away. And once I check with Kharun, I'll let you know about getting together.''

She disconnected, then punched in the familiar number at the newspaper. She tried to calculate the time difference. It would be evening there, but she suspected Pete would still be hanging around.

Sure enough, he picked up on the second ring.

"Where the hell is your story?" he blurted when he heard her voice.

"I don't have a story," Sara replied, beginning to explain how she'd been caught without getting the photographs or interviews.

"Don't give me that, babe, you are the story. Did you know going over you'd end up married to the guy? Was that part of the plan? Give the details. We're getting killed in the ratings. Every other damn paper out there is scooping us left and right—and one of our reporters is actually part of the scene. Give."

"There's nothing to say, Pete. And I'm quitting. I can't work for you anymore."

"Hey, babe, you owe me. I gave you a job without any experience. Gave you a chance to scoop the world with some photo snaps of one of the world's most eligible bachelors. I could have sent someone else. Give with some details! What's it like living in the lap of luxury? Does anyone speak English? Are you in a harem?"

"For heaven's sake, Pete, you make it sound like I've gone back to the Dark Ages. Most of Kamtansin is as modern as Algiers. There are some lovely old mosques and buildings, small tiny streets with a lot of traffic, and the people are friendly. I haven't had a chance to do much shopping, but I bet there are some real bargains to be found. I am not in a harem. Kharun has a beautiful villa right on the Mediterranean Sea."

"So if you're not a prisoner, why not contact me?

We've been waiting for a week for some news. That country's hot—with the proposed new oil leases and the potential for more.''

''It's also pretty, but deprived in many ways. That's why the oil leases are so crucial. The new income will enable them to progress more rapidly. Not that everyone is in agreement over that. But it doesn't matter, family rules over here.''

''Your guy's rich, the country's poor, what else?''

''Stop, Pete. I'm not giving a report. I called to tell you to stop calling my mother.''

''Give me your number then. I don't like one of my reporters being out of touch.''

''Didn't you hear me, I quit! You can't call here.'' Sara looked up—Kharun stood in the doorway watching her.

''I've got to go, goodbye.'' She disconnected and looked at him wondering how to explain.

''Your mother is welcome to call anytime she wishes,'' he said mildly.

Flustered she tried to smile. Not for anything did she want him to know she was speaking with her editor. He'd be convinced she still planned to do a story!

CHAPTER EIGHT

"Um, my mother wants to know when we are available to have dinner with them," Sara said, hoping her flustered feeling didn't show. "I knew it wouldn't be long before she invited us."

Kharun tilted his head slightly, his eyes studying her. "Whenever you would like."

"In a couple of days, then?"

"Fine. You took longer than I expected with your call. My mother needs to leave soon for an appointment and she wishes to discuss your taking more pictures with a view to working to devise a campaign for promoting our country."

"Do you think I can take that quality of pictures? Wouldn't a professional be better?"

"What do you think?"

She almost held her breath. Had she finally found something she was good at? "I'd give it my best shot. But I'm really a novice at this. Photography has always been a hobby."

"The quality of the pictures is assured by the camera you have. It's the composition and artistic eye that captures the essence of what you see. Your unique perspective will insure the attraction of the pictures."

"You're good for a woman's ego," she said, warming with a heartfelt glow at his praise.

"By speaking the truth?"

"By bolstering my courage to try."

"That is within you, Sara. Come, arrange things with my mother. I have work to do. Shall we ride this afternoon at five?"

"I'd like that."

The day passed swiftly. Sara went with Angelique when she left for Staboul, catching a ride to the Samin Industries headquarters.

Meeting up again with Jasmine was an eye-opener for Sara. The tall building in the heart of the business section housed several businesses owned and run by the Samin family, from shipping lines to oil exploration to import-export. The latter was headed by Jasmine herself.

"Mother said you could help with the idea we have of trying to bolster the tourist trade," Jasmine said after welcoming Sara to her office.

Glancing around the lavishly appointed office, Sara was envious. She had had a tiny cubbyhole of space at the newspaper. Nothing like the splendid view Jasmine had, nor the solid furnishings or artwork on the walls. The carpet beneath her feet was thicker than in her apartment at home!

"I'm glad to do what I can, but I don't know much about luring tourists."

Jasmine laughed. "Neither do we! But it's something my father supported. Kharun and I have badgered our uncle tirelessly until he finally told us to do what we wanted. Carte blanche is great, except that we don't have any idea how to proceed. I have one person working on it, though it technically shouldn't be done by a private firm. Still, we can get it rolling. You'll be perfect for telling us what would appeal to an American tourist—you're so new here.''

''That's what your mother said. I must say, before my father became interested in dealing for the oil leases, I hadn't heard anything about your country.''

Jasmine made a face. ''So true for everyone, I suspect. So that's a good place to start. Come, I'll introduce you to Tamil, who has started this project. Between the two of you, maybe we can really get going.''

Jasmine's enthusiasm was catching. Sara felt excited for the first time since she started work at the newspaper with such high hopes. But as she followed Jasmine to a lower floor, she began to question what she was doing. Her stay in Kamtansin wouldn't be lengthy. Once her marriage to Kharun ended, she had no reason to remain. Jasmine should have thought of that, as well—she was the only other person privy to the reason for their hasty marriage.

Before she could voice her concerns, however, Jasmine stepped into an office and introduced Sara to Tamil.

Sara was relieved to discover he spoke English, though rather slowly and formally. Still, it would facilitate working together.

By the end of the afternoon, Sara's head was swimming with ideas and plans. They had discussed various strategies and ambitions, jotted pages of notes, and arranged to meet in another couple of days to take a tour of what Tamil considered the most appealing aspects of the city to get Sara's opinions.

She was delivered back to the villa by Angelique's driver. She rang the doorbell and the same maid who had let her in before opened the door. She smiled and again said something to Sara.

''Probably telling me to get a key,'' Sara murmured as she headed for her room. Glancing at her watch, she saw it was almost five. If she wanted to be on time for her ride with Kharun, she had better hurry.

She was bubbling with all she wanted to tell him. As she donned her jeans, she almost laughed. They would be just like regular married couples—telling each other about their day.

Except, Kharun didn't tell her about his day—did he still suspect she was a spy? How absurd. Maybe if she tried—

Tried what? She sat on the edge of her bed. What did she want? To get to know Kharun better? Theirs was a temporary arrangement—to avoid scandal and make sure the oil treaties weren't jeopardized. They'd already discussed an annulment once the leases were signed.

She glanced around her room and then out at the garden, taking a deep breath. The fragrance of the flowers was light, mingling with that of the warm sea air. Her restlessness wasn't as strong when she was here. The setting was idyllic. And despite the suspicions Kharun seemed to hold, she enjoyed being with him.

Liked his kisses.

Whoa, don't go there! She jumped up and finished

changing, hurrying to the stables as if trying to flee her own thoughts.

The horses were already saddled. Kharun was talking with one of the grooms. He turned and watched as she came up to him.

"Ready?"

"As ever."

They followed the trail to the beach, Sara in the lead. Alia was prancing impatiently, anxious for the run she expected.

"Beat you!" Sara called, tearing down the beach. She could hear Kharun following, the pounding hoofs of Satin Magic drawing closer every moment. Laughing in exhilaration, Sara urged Alia faster. The wind blew through her hair, the sea sparkled like diamonds in the sun.

This is what she should capture to lure tourists. The sheer joy would entice even the most jaded traveler. How could she convey this feeling to the world?

Satin Magic was gaining. He was a strong horse, with a longer stride. Sara knew she couldn't keep her lead, but she and Alia would give it their best. Soon they were neck and neck, then Kharun pulled ahead.

Sara began to ease Alia down into a slower gait until they were trotting. Kharun slowed, turned and came back to where they were.

"You win!" Sara called.

He was grinning as he fell into step with her. "Next time, I'll win quicker with an equal start. I take it by your absence all day that you and Jasmine agreed to work together?"

"Tamil and I will be working on the project. We have so many ideas. He's traveled a bit, and so have I, so we each have ideas on what we look for and what's appealing. We need to explore hotels and restaurants and see who is ready for an influx of customers. See what tours we might devise. Decide where to target our campaign initially. There's so much to do!"

Sara was full of her day and wanted to share the excitement. She told Kharun every idea, from their plans to visit the various sights in the city of Staboul, to interviewing hotel managers, to testing restaurants. She was unaware of how her eyes sparkled in excitement, or how the color flooded her cheeks from her ride.

"Of course, what would make it perfect would be a desert trip. It's so different from what most of the world knows, I'm sure it would be a draw unto itself."

He looked at her. "You like the desert?"

"I don't know, except for my foray to try to photograph your retreat, I've never been." She patted Alia's neck. "The thought of riding a horse along the dunes has a lot of appeal. The oasis where the jail was rose so unexpectedly from the barren land. I imagine it could be romantic given the proper preparation. And you have to admit it would be quite different from what most people are used to—always supposing there's enough water and shade to support a tour group."

"Sometimes I go beyond the oasis. Satin Magic and I spend days on the desert. It is cleansing. Rejuvenating, yet relaxing."

She nodded. "I would love to see it sometime," she said wistfully. "But this is nice, along the sea. Look, there are pleasure boats out today. I haven't noticed them before—just the big ships out on the horizon.''

He glanced at the two boats apparently at anchor a few hundred yards from the shore. ''Another feature you can include. For those who sail the Med, we can offer docking facilities. We already have a couple of large marinas in Staboul. Others could be built.''

''How about docks large enough for pleasure cruises?''

''Ah, you think big. We could convert one or two of our deep water docks from freight, I suppose.''

''I can't wait to talk to Tamil about that! So I told you about my day, how was yours?'' she asked daringly. They turned the horses for home. She liked the ride back each afternoon, it was slower, took longer and allowed them to talk. Gave her time with Kharun—just the two of them. For a while she could forget he didn't trust her. For a while it was just Kharun and Sara.

She watched as he sat on his horse. His dark hair gleamed in the sunshine, his shoulders broad and strong. Savoring the image, she burned it into her memory. She never wanted to forget a single minute with him.

''I didn't realize your family was involved in so many businesses. Jasmine runs the import-export firm. Do you oversee them all?''

''You didn't know?'' he asked. Suspiciously, she thought.

She shook her head. ''I was very impressed,'' she said. ''I thought you just helped out your uncle with the oil leases and other projects he needed done.''

''My father started two of the firms. Jasmine and I

started the import-export. She assumed full control when our father died. By then I was heavily involved in the shipping lines, and now oversee the other company, as well. It's a family concern. Some cousins are involved. And my mother takes an interest, though not an active role.''

"No wonder you work all the time," she murmured.

"When a person enjoys what he does, it's not a hardship."

"What do you do for fun?" Sara asked as they neared the path leading back to the stables. Was their ride coming to an end so soon? She wanted to cling to the moments, stretch them out.

"I enjoy riding."

"How about swimming? You've never gone once since I've been here. Living right by the sea, having that lovely pool, I'd think you'd take advantage of the water."

"Ah, but I do. I usually swim first thing in the mornings, while you're still sleeping."

"Oh."

They turned into the path, going single file, Kharun in the lead. Sara watched him as they rode quietly, wondering if it would look suspiciously obvious if she arose early the next morning and happened to wish to go swimming.

"Do you ever swim at night?" she called.

He looked over his shoulder, his dark eyes enigmatic. "Sometimes. Want to go tonight?"

Her heart skipped a beat. She nodded.

"After dinner, we can take a walk. If the warmth

holds, we'll swim in the sea,'' he said. His voice was rife with sensual promise, his eyes captivating.

Sara felt the heat rise in her cheeks, but smiled slowly, hoping the sheer joy she felt didn't show. ''I'd like that.''

Sara wondered if their walk would take place when they reached the house and found Piers waiting for Kharun.

''It's late,'' Kharun said when greeting his friend and adviser. ''Couldn't whatever you're here for have waited until morning?''

Piers shrugged, looked at Sara. ''You never minded before.''

''Things change,'' Kharun answered shortly. He lifted Sara's hand and kissed it blatantly. ''Change for dinner. I'll see to Piers.''

Sara was aware of the men watching her as she headed for her wing of the house. She paused just around the bend and stopped.

''You play a dangerous game, my friend,'' she heard Piers say in English. His voice grew fainter as they moved away from her. ''You still don't know for sure she wasn't sent as a spy. Does she have access to your office?''

She knew he didn't trust her. How did Kharun really feel? His voice was too indistinct from the distance. Maybe he'd even switched to Arabic. With a sigh, she continued to her room.

Kharun closed the door to his office. ''Do you have reasons for thinking she is here to spy? A woman who speaks no Arabic and has yet to ask one question about our position on the oil leases?"

"It's just odd she showed up at this particular time, that's all."

Kharun shrugged. "What is so important you have to come this late?"

"I believe the Americans have agreed to your last counteroffer. We should go over it all in great detail, but I believe we are almost ready for you to send the version to your uncle for his approval. Then we can sign."

Kharun nodded, his expression schooled to show no emotion. *It was too soon.* He shook his head. They'd been working on this deal for weeks now. The new leases would mean a great deal to his country.

But it would also mean the need to be married to Sara would end. And he wasn't ready for that. Not yet.

"I thought you would be elated," Piers murmured, drawing out the thick folder from his briefcase.

"I'm pleased," Kharun said. "But let's make sure before we begin to celebrate. No use anticipating."

But it was clear when he read the counteroffer acceptance that the contracts were almost ready to be drawn and signed.

"It doesn't look like anything Sara could have told her father has changed our position on this," Kharun said.

"Doesn't mean they didn't try, that's all I'm saying. So, is it an annulment, or divorce?"

Kharun looked at his friend, his eyes cold and hard. "You'll be one of the first to know—when the time is right."

"Sorry, I didn't mean to overstep my bounds," Piers said hastily.

Kharun was still considering the question, and the possible answer when he changed for dinner. He had Aminna set the table on the patio overlooking the garden. After dinner, he and Sara would take that walk along the beach, and maybe go swimming.

The more he grew to know her, the more she fascinated him. Was it her quicksilver mind, flitting from one topic to another that entertained? Or the way she had of looking at him sometimes like he was the most important person in the world, that he found so beguiling? Or that air of innocence she portrayed so well?

Maybe Piers had been correct, she'd come to seduce him into revealing secrets. Yet she'd made no overt attempts at seduction. He wanted to believe she had been caught up in circumstances. Nothing so far had shown him differently.

Sara dressed with care for dinner. The sundress she donned was her favorite, loose and flowing, yet clinging as she walked, displaying her figure to full advantage. She felt she needed all the advantage she could get. Time was growing short.

She'd resented being forced into this marriage of convenience. But it had turned out to be much more pleasant than she'd expected. Granted she would change some things if she could, but for the most part she was satisfied with avoiding the scandal, which would have reflected so poorly on her father.

She had not counted on developing such an interest in her husband, however. Would he want to continue to see her after they parted?

A pang struck her. What if he didn't?

"All the more reason to make memories while I can," she said, staring at herself in the mirror. She dabbed on a hint of perfume, and recapped the bottle. Taking a deep breath, she turned and headed for dinner.

A most romantic setting, she thought, stepping into the patio after Aminna told her where to find Kharun when she found the dining room empty.

Discreet lighting gave soft illumination. The breeze had died down. The air was redolent with the fragrance of roses. And the soft murmur of the sea made a soft, melodic background.

The small table had been set with gleaming silverware, sparkling crystal. Candles shimmered, their flames dancing, reflected in Kharun's dark eyes.

"You look lovely," he said softly, reaching out his hand.

Sara slipped hers into his, feeling the shock of awareness that always took her by surprise when he touched her. Her heart pounded, and her skin grew tight with sensitivity and longing.

"Let's eat, then we'll take that walk," he said, seating her.

Dinner flew by. Sara was aware of every second, wondering what the future held. Not endless days ahead, but later tonight. Would their walk draw them even closer? Would he kiss her again?

She could scarcely eat, despite the wonderful aromas and tastes of the meal Aminna had prepared.

Kharun spoke of cities he'd visited when he lived in America, and she told him about growing up with a father who traveled the world. They shared their favorite places in Paris, and their love for riding, arguing the various merits of different breeds of horses.

By the time they finished eating, she was a bundle of nerves. Always in the back of her mind had been the promised walk. Alone with Kharun in the dark, along the sea.

Kharun looked at her gravely. "What's wrong?"

"Nothing."

He didn't look as if the answer satisfied, so she continued. "I'm still excited about the plans Tamil and I made today. I can't wait until tomorrow when we look around the city."

He nodded, his eyes narrowed. "Shall we take that walk?"

She blew out her breath and smiled. "I'd like that."

The moon was full, providing enough light to clearly see the path, bathing the white sand with enough illumination to clearly see their way. Sara stopped when they reached the beach to slip off her sandals.

"I like going barefoot," she said, looping them with one finger.

"Be careful where you step. There are broken shells sometimes," he warned, taking her free hand.

She almost shivered at the sensations that tingled along her arm. Glancing around, she almost didn't recognize the beach as the place she'd visited several mornings.

An air of mystery hovered. The sea was dark, the anchor lights of the pleasure crafts the only break in the blackness. The silvery sheen of the sand added to her pleasure, evoking dreams of romantic settings and faithful lovers.

Kharun began angling toward the water, his presence compelling.

"I think I'd come out every night if I lived here," Sara murmured.

"You do live here."

"Temporarily. How are the lease discussions coming?"

He hesitated a moment. She glanced at him.

"They are progressing. How does your father feel about them?"

"I don't know. I haven't spoken to him since our wedding. I did talk to my mother again and arranged for us to have dinner with them tomorrow night, if that's all right with you. Will that be awkward, you and my father sitting down to dinner when you are on opposite sides of negotiations?"

"We are not enemies, Sara. We both want these leases, we're just hammering out the details."

"Mom doesn't like business discussions at the table," she warned.

"A wise woman. I enjoyed meeting her. Are you worried about having dinner with them?"

"A bit. What if they suspect this is all a sham?"

"What would happen?"

She sighed. "They'd be disappointed. I'm a trial to them, I suspect."

"I doubt it. From what I saw, they seemed to delight in your company."

"That's because you saw them at the wedding—when they were predisposed to be happy. Someone else finally took me off their hands."

"Do you think they feel that way? At first they were bewildered. But when they thought you were happy, they were happy."

"So they'll be even more disappointed when the truth comes out. Not that that's your worry."

"We don't have to end the marriage the day we sign the agreements, you know," he said slowly.

"We don't?"

Kharun stopped and turned her so she faced him. He released her hand and placed his on her shoulders. "Piers suggested it might be a slap in the face to the ministers to end it immediately by annulment. We'd be essentially telling them all we'd played a trick."

"Oh." For some reason his rationale depressed her. She'd thought when he first spoke he wanted to keep their arrangement a little longer. Now it was further expediency, nothing more.

"So what do you think?"

"Whatever." She couldn't think with Kharun's hands toying with her hair, his thumbs caressing her jaw. She could only feel the myriad sensations that filled her, that heated her blood and had her longing for things never known.

"I was thinking—"

"What?" She tried breathing normally, every nerve cell at attention and craving more.

"Maybe an annulment isn't such a good idea. A divorce might be more persuasive."

Her heart pounded so hard she wondered if he could see it. Blood pulsed like thunder through her veins. She peered up at him, trying to determine what he was saying—what he really meant.

"A divorce?"

"It is customary when ending a marriage that has been consummated," he said, leaning down to kiss her.

CHAPTER NINE

HE WAS kissing her. He wanted more. More than kisses. Rational thought fled as touch turned her knees wobbly and her thought processes to mush.

He wanted her. Every brush of his lips, stroke of his tongue, caress of his fingertips shouted the message loud and clear.

And she wanted him. Wanted to be closer still, to explore all the cravings that filled her body. Wanted to touch him all over, learn every secret he had to share.

When he pulled back to look at her, she smiled. "I think a divorce is the only way to go," she said huskily.

He swept her up into his arms, her strong desert raider, and turned for the house. She encircled his neck, cherishing every moment. What woman hadn't dreamed of a man sweeping her off her feet since seeing Rhett sweep Scarlet up the steps in *Gone With the Wind*? Was anything more romantic?

Only to have it happen to her.

She scarcely noticed when they reached the garden, except she could see him better with the illumination of the garden lights. He followed the path to her room, entering through the opened French doors.

The soft twinkling from the garden gave all the light they needed. Setting her beside the bed, he took her sandals and dropped them on the floor.

"Are you sure, Sara? There'll be no going back," he said, caressing her cheek.

Her heart exploded with love for this enigmatic man before her. She didn't know him well, but she knew he was honorable and caring. Theirs was an odd arrangement, doomed to end before long. But she loved him as she'd never loved another.

When had that happened?

Could the feelings she had truly be love? Yet what was more natural than a woman wanting to share all she could with the man she loved?

"I'm so very sure, Kharun." So saying, she reached up and pulled his head down for a kiss.

Taking liberties she would never have dared even a day before, she threaded her fingers in his thick hair, relishing her right to touch him.

His hands roamed over her back, pressing her against his hard body, lifting her slightly to bring her even closer. Heat built as his clever fingers found the fastenings for her dress and released them. The cool air on her back should have startled, but she was too caught up in the roiling excitement that grew with each feather stroke of his fingers.

The world spun when he lifted her to place her on the bed. Then it righted itself as he joined her.

Sara awoke when Kharun left her. Dawn was breaking. He was going for his swim, she knew it. For an instant, she considered throwing back the light covering and joining him. But tendrils of passion still filled her, and she wanted to savor the feelings a bit longer. She smiled dreamily and drifted back to sleep hugging the pillow he'd used, breathing in his special scent.

By the time Sara awoke for the day, the sun was high in the sky. Slowly she bathed and dressed. Wondering where Kharun was, she headed for the dining room. Only to be disappointed when it was empty—save for a place set at the table and some food warming on the sideboard. She poured a cup of coffee and selected a couple of croissants. Stepping outside, she went to sit in the shade.

Last night had been beyond her wildest dreams. They'd made love more than once and each time was like it had been invented just to join Kharun and Sara forever.

Wryly she acknowledged he likely didn't feel the same way. The thought threatened to overwhelm her. It was enough she'd had a night with him. Maybe more nights to come. But she'd entered this arrangement with her head fully aware of the consequences. She'd see her commitment through and leave when the time came. She just hoped she was able to leave without clinging, without asking for more than Kharun ever promised to give.

Aminna stepped into the doorway.

"His Excellency said to tell you he had to go to the city today. He will meet you at the hotel for dinner with your parents at seven."

Sara tried to smile, but her hopes and dreams vanished in an instant. Confirmation that last night hadn't meant as much to him as it had to her. Not with such a cryptic message. Not with leaving her alone all day. Leaving without even seeking her out to say goodbye in person.

Without another kiss.

"Thank you. I will be going to the city myself today." At least she still had the appointment with Tamil. How she would have faced the day without that, she didn't know.

"What time? I'll inform the driver."

"I need to be at the company headquarters at ten."

Aminna bowed slightly and left Sara to her rueful thoughts.

By the time seven o'clock rolled around, Sara had been through more emotional turmoil than she cared to repeat anytime soon. She vacillated from being understanding of the demands of Kharun's time and work to being convinced he'd used them as a mere excuse to escape.

She went right up to her parents' suite and knocked on the door a few minutes before seven. Might as well get this over with, and hope for the best.

"Sara!" Her mother swept her into her arms for a brief hug, then held her back, studying her daughter.

"You look radiant."

Sara was startled. Did she? Or was her mother seeing only what she wanted to see?

"Just like a new bride should look. Come in, and tell me all about being married to Kharun. I imagine it would be vastly different from your father."

"One type A personality is similar to another," Sara said, smiling at her mother.

"Ah, but your father wasn't always like that. We married right out of college. We were both so young. But Kharun is already established as a man of the world—

not only in running several international businesses, but negotiating oil treaties on behalf of his country. Vastly different from the early days of our marriage.''

"I guess," Sara said, struck by the difference.

They moved into the sitting room area of the suite and settled on the luxurious sofas.

"Before I forget, though I doubt there's a danger of that, your obnoxious boss keeps calling, demanding to talk to you. He really is getting tiresome."

"Pete? I called him after you told me of his calls. He's still bothering you?"

"Persistent, I have to give him that."

"Can you ignore him? Just hang up the next time he calls, maybe that'll get through to him."

"Actually, I have the front desk screening our calls now. Tiresome, but at least I haven't spoken directly with him today. Ah, here's your father."

"Sara." Samuel Kinsale entered from the adjoining room. He hugged her when she rose, then held her away from him, his hands on her shoulders, studying her.

"Marriage seems to agree with you," he said. Glancing around, he frowned. "Where's Kharun?"

Just then there was a tap at the outer door.

"That's probably him now. He was coming from the office," Sara said, crossing to the door. Her heart skipped a beat in anticipation.

She opened the door, struck anew by Kharun's sexy looks. Her breath caught when he swept her into his arms and kissed her deeply. When he pulled back a moment later, she wanted to grab hold and never let him go.

Startled by the trend of her thoughts, she smiled shakily and stepped back, as if putting distance between them could erase her wanton desires.

"Hi," she said breathlessly.

He smiled that lazy smile then looked beyond her to her parents.

"Good evening."

"Kharun, good to see you."

Samuel and Roberta greeted their guest with obvious warmth. Before long, Roberta had everyone comfortable and at ease.

"No talking shop tonight," she warned the others. "This is a family dinner, not some negotiating session!"

Samuel laughed and nodded. "Very well. Kharun and I get enough negotiating. Tell me, how are you enjoying married life?"

Kharun glanced at Sara then looked at her father. "It is different from what I expected, but it has its compensations."

She pasted an insipid smile on her face and hoped her thoughts weren't reflected. Marriage wasn't what he expected because it was a farce. He deserved to marry a woman he cared about, not to cover up a scandal that might prove an embarrassment to his country.

The comment about compensation didn't go unnoticed. Was that all last night had been to him, a form of compensation for the sacrifice he'd made?

Her head held high, Sara tried to maintain the facade of a radiant bride, happy with life. But she longed for privacy. Even her room at Kharun's villa would be preferable to being with her parents now and trying to keep up appearances with people who knew her so well.

And Kharun didn't help matters. He was sitting far too close. She could feel his thigh against hers, and his shoulder brushed hers when he leaned forward to put his glass on the table. Settling back, he put his arm around her shoulders, his hand lightly tracing circles against the sensitive skin in her upper arm.

She could hardly concentrate on the conversation. Every fiber of her being was attuned to the sensations sweeping through her from his touch. How was anyone supposed to remain coherent when all they could think about was getting alone with the man and seeing if they could take up where they'd left off the night before?

She flicked a quick look at her mother. Roberta was serenely responding to one of Kharun's questions. She didn't seem to notice anything amiss. But Sara felt the entire world had to be able to hear her rapid heartbeat, feel the heat that suffused, know she was focused on Kharun to the exclusion of everything else.

Dinner seemed interminable. She kept her eyes on her plate, lest she give away her emotional turmoil and stare at Kharun for endless moments. Once or twice, when addressed directly, she looked up. Each time Kharun's warm gaze rested on her.

It was all for show. To put on a good front before her parents, to pretend to the world that everything was fine.

Suddenly Sara wished with all her heart it wasn't a charade. That they were married forever and could go home together when the evening ended and close the rest of the world out of their special place.

She stared at the last of the food on her plate. *She'd fallen in love with a man who didn't trust her!* A man who found her a problem to be dealt with and then summarily dismissed once the situation was resolved. Not the best move she'd ever made. Nothing had gone the way she'd expected since she stepped foot onto Kamtansin soil.

She reached for her water and took a long drink, wishing she could catch the next plane home.

She couldn't stay. She'd give herself away any instant, and she couldn't bear the humiliation of his knowing the awkward, flaky daughter of Samuel Kinsale had fallen in love with one of the world's most powerful men.

At least when she made mistakes, they were terrific ones. No little namby-pamby ones for her.

She should have been better prepared. Should have guarded her heart against his appeal and attraction.

What she should have done was refused to go riding with him, ignored his family, fought him at every turn and demanded she be allowed to leave.

Now she didn't ever want to leave, yet the days were counting down and it was only a matter of time before he'd ask her to. Their marriage facade would no longer be needed once the leases were signed. Her ideas for tourism might be utilized, but her presence wouldn't be required.

She could hardly keep from jumping up and screaming at the unfairness of it all. For the first time she'd found someone she truly loved, and it was not meant to be.

"Are you all right?" Kharun asked.

Sara looked up. "Fine."

His eyes narrowed as he studied her. Thankfully, she knew he could not read minds. But his steady regard was making her nervous.

She wasn't fine, she'd made the biggest mess of her life. But she'd bluff her way through. The entire sequence of events was her fault. She would not add to it by letting him suspect her feelings had changed.

The evening seemed interminable, but finally it was time to leave.

Her mother gave her a hug. "I like him so much. I hope you'll always be happy."

Sara smiled, feeling as if a knife was twisting in her heart. What would her mother say in a few weeks, when the marriage was over? Sara didn't even want to think about it.

"You were silent tonight," Kharun said as they settled in the back of the limousine and headed for the villa. "Are you usually so quiet in the presence of your parents?"

"What? Oh, no. We talk a lot, actually."

"So I was the damper on the evening?"

She shook her head, trying to see him in the darkness. The ride reminded her of that first ride from the jail in the desert. She'd never in a million years suspected she'd end up loving the man beside her.

When they reached the villa, Kharun held his hand out for hers to assist her from the car. He didn't release it and Sara tried unsuccessfully to tug free. She didn't need any closer proximity to the man. His attraction was overwhelming. Distance was what she needed.

Lights were on in the house, providing a soft illumination in the living room and halls.

Kharun raised her hand to his lips, brushing a tantalizing kiss to her wrist. "Stay the night with me," he said, his voice low and husky.

It was as if liquid heat poured through her. *He wanted her again tonight!* Dare she follow through?

She loved him, she wanted to be with him in every way. But theirs was only a temporary alliance. Could she spend the night with him and save herself from heartache?

No. But the heartache would come either way. Why not grab the chance to be with him?

"Your place or mine?"

"Tonight, mine."

He leaned over to kiss her. His mouth touched hers with a familiarity that belied the short time they'd known each other. The sensations that filled her were growing familiar with each passing second. She opened her lips to deepen their kiss, thrilled at the responsiveness he displayed.

Slowly, as if dancing to some unheard tune, he turned her and moved with easy abandonment down the long hall, away from her room and the illusion of safety it provided.

Instead, between kisses, she knew they were going to a room she had yet to see. Kharun's private retreat. His own bedroom.

When they reached the door, it stood ajar. Sara loosened her arms, locked around his neck, and peered into the dimness. She could see a bed and the gleam of light on one wall—a mirror reflecting the hallway illumination.

She looked up, into Kharun's dark gaze—alive with desire and impatience, though he kept the latter in check.

"Yes or no?" he said, as if divining uncertainty. He was giving the choice to her.

"Yes." She reached up and kissed him, trying to let him know by touch and actions how much she wanted him. How much she reveled in being with him. If she could offer nothing else, she'd be honest in this. If it had to end, then she'd make sure it ended gloriously. Maybe down through the years, Kharun would think of her once in a while—and think of what might have been.

The next morning Kharun woke early. Sara was snuggled next to him, fast asleep. For a long moment he watched her, fascinated by the hint of color in her cheeks, the sweep of her lashes against her fair skin. Slowly he ran his fingers through her hair, enjoying the shimmering color, and satiny softness. For a moment he thought he could spend the entire day just watching Sara sleep.

Then reality took hold. He had an appointment at nine, and things to see to before that. This was not the time or the place to indulge in fantasies, no matter how tempting.

Once things were resolved, however, he would find the time and place to discover more about this bewitching woman who was his wife before he'd let her go.

Piers was waiting for him when he reached the downtown offices, his face beaming.

"I think you'll be pleased with the lease terms. We've gotten everything we asked for on the last go. I'd say we're ready to sign. You just need to recommend it to your uncle and we can begin further exploration before the month is out."

"Good work."

"Your doing. Not that I want to take anything away from your negotiating skills, but marrying Sara was a stroke of genius. I'm sure some of the concessions we got were a result of her father's feeling generous in light of the marriage."

Kharun frowned. He didn't want favors like that. The relationship between him and Sara was complex. They were both walking a fine line. And after last night, and the night before, the line had blurred.

A quick finish to the business at hand. Was he ready for that? The reason for their marriage would vanish. No matter how much Garh and Hamin wished to discredit the oil deal with his uncle, once the leases were signed, it would prove a moot point.

Kharun's phone rang.

"Yes?" His secretary was on the other end. Hearing the news that Garh Sonharh was in the outer office demanding to see him, he told her to send him in.

"I suspect Garh has heard the news," he said as he hung up.

Piers looked puzzled. "He's here?"

Garh pushed open the door, pausing in the opening for dramatic impact.

"You are a fool, Kharun. It was not enough you wished to jeopardize the future of our country, but to make it possible for the paparazzi to hold us to ridicule is beyond acceptable.'' He strode into the office and tossed several faxed newspapers on the desk.

Kharun looked at the top one. It was from a tabloid newspaper from the United States. A bad photo of Sara stared back at him. The headlines screamed A Hostage To Fortune?

He looked up. ''What is this, Garh?''

''Copies of newspapers on sale in the United States. One of my people saw it, copied it and sent it to me. If your new wife is not a spy, then she certainly is a woman to make the most of her opportunities. In this case, fame and notoriety on a world-wide scale. I cannot help but think your uncle will think twice about signing a lease with a member of the opposition so bent on ridiculing us.''

''I'll deal with it,'' Kharun said evenly. He wanted to smash something—preferably Garh's face. But that would solve nothing. He had to read the newspaper article, assess the damage, then rectify the situation. But not with Garh still in the room.

''I'm taking the papers to your uncle.''

''You must do what you think is right, of course,'' Kharun said disinterestedly. He looked at Piers.

''I'll see you out,'' Piers said, quick to catch on.

Kharun watched as Piers hustled Garh from his office. Once the door was firmly shut behind them, he sat down and drew the damaging fax papers toward him. The second sheet had pictures of them riding on the beach. The caption read ''Aborted escape attempt.'' He almost laughed. The photographer had caught their race—the one where Sara had initially been leading.

The second one was on the beach. He remembered that night, the scent of her that had filled him with such desire. Her laughter, her delight in wading in the warm sea. When she'd almost stepped on a shell, he'd caught her and pulled her back. From a distance, and with the wrong interpretation, he guessed it could look as if she were trying to escape and that he'd stopped her. The pleasure crafts anchored off the beach—a clever cover for the paparazzi.

He set the sheet aside and began to read the inflaming article. Had Sara sent this in? If enough people read it and believed it, it could damage their reputation with the United States.

From the first moment, she'd been trouble. He pushed back his chair and rose. Time to get this settled once and for all.

CHAPTER TEN

SARA was sitting on the patio beside the pool sipping her last cup of coffee for the morning. The air was soft against her skin, a hint of the sea mingled with the faint fragrance of the flowers. She sat beneath an umbrella, which shaded her from the hot rays of the sun. Later she was due to meet Tamil for more discussions. But right now she had nothing to do.

Except dream. And remember.

Remember the most incredible night of her life. She wondered if Kharun had any idea how sexy he was, or how just thinking about him could set her senses spinning. Did the memory of their loving spring to mind when he was at work, or were men better able to compartmentalize their lives?

"Telephone for you," Aminna said in her heavily accented French, standing in the doorway.

Sara smiled and rose, glancing around for the portable phone. She didn't see it.

"Where shall I take it?"

"In the office." She led the way.

Sara slipped into Kharun's office and saw the phone receiver lying on the desk. Aminna nodded and left, shooing out the maid who had obviously been dusting.

"Hello?" She sank into the big chair behind the desk, feeling odd to be in Kharun's office with him not there.

"Sara, it's your mother."

"Is something wrong?" She could tell by the tone in her mother's voice something was definitely wrong.

"Your father just got a call from a friend of his in the State Department asking if you were all right."

"Why in the world would he get such a call?"

"Apparently because of a newspaper article that appeared in the U.S. yesterday."

Sara felt her blood grow cold. "A tabloid paper, run by Pete Steede?"

"With headlines implying you are being held hostage while the oil leases are being negotiated."

She muttered an expletive, heard her mother's sharp gasp. She was going to kill Pete! How dare he exploit her life just to sell newspapers! Immediately she thought of Kharun.

"How bad is it?" she asked.

"Your father is getting a copy of the article faxed through. We'll know more then, but it was bad enough for his friend to call to make sure you were all right. You need to verify this with him. Can you call Paul Michaels yourself and tell him it's a mix-up? I've got his phone number right here. Needless to say, your father isn't really happy about this."

"Neither am I!" And she knew for darn sure Kharun would be furious. Especially if it ever got back to this country and the ministers who were so opposed to the oil leases saw the newspaper. Fortunately the tabloid was limited to U.S. distribution.

"His phone number—"

"Wait, I need to find paper and a pencil." She opened

the top drawer of the desk. Neat and tidy, nothing like her own back at work. A workplace she would never see again, unless it was to go and wring Pete's neck.

She picked up a pen. There was no paper.

She closed it and opened the top right drawer.

"Looking for something?" The cold voice at the door stopped her instantly.

She looked up into Kharun's glittering eyes. He was angry. Any idiot could see that.

"I'll call you back," she told her mother, and clicked the phone off.

"Why call back? Why not find what you're looking for while he waits?"

"He? That was my mother."

His patent look of disbelief riled her.

"It was! Call her back yourself if you don't believe me. She wanted to give me a phone number. I was looking for something to write on."

"Try this," he said, tossing the faxed copies of the newspaper article onto the desk.

Sara swallowed hard as she recognized the headline banner. Oh, God, he knew!

Knew and was furious.

She licked her lips nervously. "How did you get a copy?"

He tilted his head slightly. "From Garh Sonharh."

Slowly Sara drew the papers closer. She groaned when she saw the photos and captions. But anger grew as she read the inflammatory article. No wonder Kharun was so furious.

"I didn't write this," she said, standing. "You don't believe I did, do you?"

"Wrote it, collaborated, dictated—it makes no difference. No one but you could have provided all the information—where the villa is, when we would be riding, the hurried wedding, tension between family members. No one but you."

"I didn't do it. Pete did."

"He conjured it up out of thin air?"

She hesitated, but she couldn't let Kharun think she'd betray him. "I talked to him once. But only once. He kept calling—"

"What are you doing in this office?" he interrupted, obviously not interested in her explanation.

"Aminna said I could take the call here. It was my mother. She was giving me a phone number to call and I needed something to write it down on." She drew a deep breath. "I'm not spying on you if that's what you think."

"I'm not sure what I think right now."

"Fine, let me know when you decide." Head held high, she swept from the room, going wide around Kharun as if suspecting he'd try to stop her.

But he said nothing. Made no move.

She didn't know whether to be angry at him or not. She knew she was furious with Pete. She walked back out onto the patio. Her coffee was cold. The pool mocked her with its memories of another time.

She spun around and headed for her room. Snatching up her purse, she left. She'd visit her parents and get to the bottom of this. And she'd call Pete Steede from the privacy of her parents' suite.

Hesitating only a second as she left the villa, she wished Kharun had believed her. Had stood by her. But why should he? She'd messed this up like she did everything.

Yet it was a thousand times worse this time. She loved him. She would never do anything to cause him harm. But would he ever come to see her as anyone but the aggravating woman who threw a wrench into the smooth workings of his negotiations? And how had that blasted article affected his relationship with his uncle's ministers?

She looked at the villa one last time. Would she ever come back?

Highly unlikely.

Kharun's car was parked in front, his chauffeur seated in the driver's seat, reading.

She opened the back door and ignored his start of surprise.

"Presentation Hotel," she said, settling in as if she had every right to do so. She prayed he'd comply and not verify her destination with Kharun. The sooner she was away the better.

He nodded, tossed aside the newspaper and started the car.

In moments, she was on her way. It was hard not to look back. Harder still to keep the tears at bay. But it was better this way. Better to leave him, try to clear up the mess Steede had caused and then stay with her parents until the leases were signed, sealed and delivered.

*   *   *

"What the hell do you mean she's gone?" Kharun roared. Aminna stood in the doorway, her face impassive despite his anger.

"Sargon drove her to the Presentation Hotel."

"He didn't check with me first?"

"Why should he? She is your wife. She needed a ride. He has returned and is waiting to take you back to your office when you are ready."

Kharun ran his fingers through his hair and tried to think. His thought processes were short-circuited— thanks to Sara Kinsale bak Samin. Like they had been almost since he met her. Now this.

Conclusive evidence she'd betrayed him? Or just a woman prudently staying out of range until his anger cooled?

Think!

For all he knew, she and her mother had been making lunch plans on the phone.

If she'd been speaking with her mother.

He hated not knowing what to believe.

The phone rang again. He'd been fielding calls ever since Garh had left his office—no doubt to spread the word about the tabloid article. Kharun had already placated his uncle, and Hamin. And his aunt. At least he thought he'd placated his aunt. Time would tell.

In the meantime, he needed to see Sara.

He nodded to Aminna and paced to the window, trying to think. In retrospect, maybe he should have followed Piers's advice way back at the beginning. Shipped her off somewhere and not told a soul.

An idea glimmered. Slowly Kharun began to relax. He'd give Sara until tonight. If she didn't return, then he'd go to get her.

"I don't understand, Sara."

"Mom, just trust me on this, okay?"

"But you didn't bring a suitcase or anything. How can you plan to stay the night? What would Kharun say?"

"He'll be glad to have me out of his hair."

"What? Will you explain? Ever since you got here this morning, you've done little more than make two phone calls and pace around on the carpet so much I think it's wearing thin. You didn't eat enough dinner to keep a bird alive."

"The carpet's fine."

"But you're not."

Sara looked at her mother and almost gave way to tears. But she kept them in. She'd made the mess she was in, and it was up to her to get herself out. She couldn't keep running to Mommy.

"I'm fine."

Roberta shook her head. "I know, you don't want to talk about it. Fine. But I'm here if you need me. And so is your father."

"Thanks." Sara smiled as best she could, and paced to the window. Her father had not been at dinner, finishing up some things, he'd told his wife. At least she'd been spared having to talk to him about the stupid article.

Her conversation with Pete had been less than satisfactory. There was no changing the newspaper once it hit the stands. Now there was only damage control. And a promise to sue him to kingdom come if he didn't print a retraction.

Not that it would do much good. Retractions were never front-page headlines.

Her father entered the suite. "Hello, Sara, I didn't know you were here. But you can hear the news when I tell your mother."

Roberta greeted her husband. "What news?"

"The leases were approved this afternoon. We lost a few concessions thanks to Kharun's tough negotiations, but we now have the exclusive rights for the next ten years. Work will start before the end of the month."

"Darling, that's wonderful! Does that mean we can go home soon?"

"As soon as next week."

Sara felt as if she'd been struck. It was over. There was no reason to continue their marriage. She almost laughed. There'd be no reason for Kharun to seek her out tonight, or wonder where she was. He was probably congratulating himself that he didn't even have to tell her to go, she'd left on her own.

"That's great, Dad," she said brightly. Her face was going to crack if she didn't get away from her parents. She could only fake a smile for so long.

"I'm tired. I think I'll go to bed. Good night."

"What's going on?" Samuel asked as she fled the room.

"I'm not sure," her mother replied just as Sara shut

the door to the room she'd used her first night in Kamtansin.

Leaning against the cool wood, Sara let the tears well into her eyes, wishing the pain in her heart would ease enough to let her find oblivion in sleep.

She'd held heaven in her hands, and lost it.

"Oh, Kharun," she whispered.

He hadn't called, hadn't made any effort to even find her, much less ask her to return home. Now that the leases were approved, there was no reason to see him again.

But she wanted to. Wished she could be with him forever. Explain, make sure he knew she had not betrayed him, that she'd lived up to her commitment.

A knock sounded on the door to the hallway. She pushed away from the door connecting to the sitting room of the suite and crossed the spacious bedroom. Was it the maid to turn down the bed?

She opened the door, shocked to see two uniformed men standing there.

"Sara Kinsale?" one asked.

"Yes."

"Please come with us."

"Who are you? Where do you want me to go?"

"Please come with us."

The second man reached out to take her arm in a firm grasp, pulling her from the room.

"Wait!" She had to tell her parents. She couldn't just disappear. Not again.

The door was pulled shut behind them and they headed down the hall. For a moment, she experienced déjà vu—of a guard holding her arm at the jail in the desert. Was she being returned to jail? Had Kharun reneged on his promise to her because he thought she'd betrayed him with Pete?

"I can't go with you," she said, trying to pull free.

His grip was too solid.

When they bypassed the regular elevators and took the freight elevator, she began to get scared. Her parents didn't know she wasn't in her room. It would be morning before they discovered it. Where would she be?

Before she knew it she was seated between the two men in a fast-moving car. It headed away from the city. Into the desert.

Sara's thoughts swirled. She had to get away, get to a phone.

Call the American embassy? she thought hysterically. Where were they going? And why?

The night was dark once the city lights were left behind. Only the slash of the headlights of the car cut through the impenetrable darkness. Sara gave up demanding to know what was happening. She suspected only the one man knew any English and that sounded very basic.

Despite her worry, she was growing tired. It had been a long day. Emotionally she was exhausted. The monotony of riding through the darkness began to wear her down. Slowly her eyes closed.

Before she could fall asleep, however, the car began to slow.

Snapping open her eyes, she stared around her. Nothing to be seen in the dark. The star-studded sky ended in the far horizon into inky blackness. No lights shone, no buildings were silhouetted against the night sky.

The car stopped and the driver said something in Arabic. The man to her right opened his door and stepped out, motioning for Sara.

She slowly scooted across the seat and stood. The air was warm, a light breeze blowing. But the scent of the sea was missing. This was dry, clear air.

"Why did we stop?"

"We wait," he said.

"For what?"

He shrugged, reached for a cigarette and lit it.

Sara leaned against the car, wondering if she dare try to make a run. She had no idea where she was, or how far from Staboul they were. But the faint glow back from where they came showed her where the city was. On foot it might not take her longer than four or five days' walking.

Her shoes weren't up to it, though the long pants would keep sunburn at bay. She was getting goofy, she thought. She would have no chance to walk back to Staboul—she had no water.

She heard a drumming sound and looked around, trying to figure out what it was, and from where it was coming.

A horse. What was a horse doing out here in the middle of nowhere?

It was coming closer. The man put out his cigarette and said something to the man in the car. The engine started again.

Sara turned to get back into the vehicle, but he stopped her. "No, you wait." He climbed inside and closed the door. The driver turned on his headlights.

Turning to face the direction of the sound, Sara waited, wondering what was next. In only a moment she saw the horse and rider outlined against the stars. The horse looked huge, and the rider was dressed in traditional Arab garb, complete with a folded scarf across his face. Only his eyes were visible in the glow of the headlights.

She reached for the door handle. She didn't want to be left out here at the mercy of some desert raider. Was she to be spirited away, never to be heard from again?

But the car was locked. Once the men saw the rider, the car began to pull away.

Sara felt as if her last hope was disappearing.

The horse took a step forward, another. The rider had said nothing. Sara's heart began to beat rapidly. Glancing on either side, she could see no shelter, no place to hide.

"Come." The man reached out a hand.

Sara took a step back. "I don't think so."

"No adventure?"

She stopped, stared. "Kharun?"

"Come."

She couldn't believe her ears. Was it him? But what would he be doing out in the middle of nowhere? She tried to see if the horse was Satin Magic, but it was too dark.

"Come." The hint of impatience convinced her. She'd recognize that tone anywhere.

She reached up and in seconds sat sideways in front of him. She was barely in place before he drew her close and turned the horse around. Then they were flying across the desert.

She hoped he knew where they were going. Not that it mattered. It was exhilarating, riding along the vast empty space, the wind in her face, the stars like distant diamonds overhead, Kharun's arms tightly around her. She closed her eyes, savoring every moment, committing everything to memory. This was an experience she never wanted to forget.

Sara wasn't certain how long they rode, but when he began to slow, she looked around. No sounds met her ears, except the jingle of the horse's bridle. No building rose.

"Where are we?" she asked.

Kharun pulled the horse to a stop and eased her to the ground, coming to stand beside her a moment later.

"A place where no one else will find us."

She looked at him. "No one?" She almost squeaked it out.

"You said you wanted to see the desert, I've brought you." Swiftly he unsaddled the horse, and tethered him.

He took her arm gently in one hand and led her around a low mound.

"Wait here a minute." He lifted the flap to the large tent and entered. In only seconds, a warm glow emanated.

Sara lifted the flap and followed without waiting for Kharun.

The inside stunned her. Rich Persian carpets covered

the ground. Tapestries hung from the back wall, their vibrant colors reflecting the lamplight. A large bed was erected on one side, draped in gauzy netting. The center brass table gleamed in the light, fruits and nuts heaped in bowls.

"Wow." She lifted her gaze to Kharun. He stood like a bold desert raider in the midst of the splendor. His robes swirled around him as he turned and stared at her, his hands on his hips. The covering from his face was gone, but the rest was pure Arabian fantasy. Her heart skipped into high gear. Her blood raced through her veins faster than ever. She was almost light-headed.

He'd been angry when last she'd seen him.

He didn't look angry now.

Involuntarily her gaze moved to the bed.

"All the comforts of home," she said. She'd meant to be sarcastic. Instead the throaty sound of her voice was sultry, enticing, sexy. Slowly she smiled, hoping he didn't guess how nervous she was.

"Why are we here?" she asked.

"Time alone, just the two of us. The negotiations are concluded."

"I heard. So our marriage is over?"

He tilted his head slightly, then drew the headpiece off and carelessly tossed it to a cushion. His dark hair was mussed. Sara's fingers almost ached with desire to tousle his hair even more, to touch him, feel his heat and strength.

"So, do you mind telling me what we're doing here?" she asked.

"You haven't seen the desert. I wouldn't want you to

go home without experiencing all of my country's delights.''

The primary delight she'd experienced in this country was being with Kharun, but Sara couldn't say that out loud.

''Aren't you worried I'll take photos and send them to the newspaper? Or report some nefarious deeds?''

He laughed, his teeth startling white when compared to his tanned skin. ''You said you didn't write that article.''

''Nor dictate nor collaborate. You seem to be taking this better now than this morning.''

''Perhaps,'' he said, motioning to one of the cushions near the brass table. ''Care to sit?''

She watched him warily for a moment, then nodded, moving to sink on the soft pillow. It felt a bit awkward, but was comfortable. She looked at the food on the table, at the lamp, anywhere but at Kharun.

He sat beside her, crowding her. He could have sat opposite. Did it mean something that he hadn't?

''How did you do all this?'' she asked, sweeping her arm to indicate the tent and the accoutrements.

''I keep the tent for a retreat. It's kept clean and stocked for me. Food is kept for Satin Magic, as well. When I want to use it, I let the caretaker know, and he disappears until I leave.''

''So we really are alone in the middle of the desert?''

''We really are all alone. Does that concern you?'' He leaned closer. Sara could feel the heat from his body envelop her. His breath caressed her cheeks as she looked up into his dark eyes. Her own breath caught.

"No." It came out almost a whisper.

"Good." He closed the distance between them and kissed her.

Reality faded and fantasy took hold. His touch was all she'd ever dreamed of, inflaming her senses, building desire and passion to blend with the love she already felt growing and encompassing her entire being.

She returned his kiss, meeting him halfway, reveling in the sensations that threatened to catapult her into a realm of hedonistic pleasure never known before.

His hand brushed back her hair as he held her face for the kisses that rained down on her. Then he forged a trail of fire and ice as he kissed and nibbled down her neck, to focus on the rapid pulse point at the base of her throat that seemed to fascinate him.

Just maybe she wasn't the only one in this fantasy.

She should be doing something practical about returning to the capital city. About arranging her trip home.

But Sara didn't feel the least bit practical. She craved his touch like she would crave water in the desert. Maybe because he was as important to her life.

"Tonight is ours," he said.

"Yes." She would agree to anything he said, as long as he kept kissing her.

But when he rose and lifted her in his arms, a moment of panic struck. It abated instantly when he pushed through the netting and laid her on the bed.

It was incredibly soft—and large. More room than the two of them needed, she thought hazily as he joined her. When he kissed her again, Sara stopped thinking. She had one last night, and she was going to enjoy every second of being with Kharun.

Dawn was breaking in the east when Kharun woke Sara with a gentle kiss.

"Um?" She burrowed closer. She didn't want to wake up. Didn't want to face the day.

"Come and see the dawn. There's nothing like it as it spreads over the desert, the light faint at first, then growing bolder. The temperature is cool—nothing like the searing heat of midday. And the shadows allow your imagination to fly."

Her imagination was flying right now, and it centered on the two of them in bed, not getting up, going into the cold dawn air.

She didn't want her last night with Kharun to end. She wanted time to stand still.

"Go away," she said grumpily. If he didn't want to stretch it out, so be it. But she could.

"Come on, you'll love it."

"I love you," she mumbled. Then froze, suddenly coming completely awake, though she kept her eyes shut. Tightly shut. Oh, she hadn't really said that out loud, had she?

She held her breath. Please, please, please, she thought, don't let me have said that out loud.

His finger tilted her face up. She kept her eyes shut.

"Sara?"

With a sigh, she slowly opened her eyes. His dark eyes stared down into hers, his expression unreadable.

"Well now that I'm awake, I might as well get up

and see that sunrise. Then we can go back to Staboul and I can make arrangements to head for home,'' she grumbled, starting to get out of bed.

Their legs were tangled, and Kharun clamped a hand on her arm. She couldn't move.

"Maybe we need to talk," he suggested.

"Maybe we need to get on with our lives," she replied. "Let me up, or the sun will beat us."

"We have a few minutes. You know the oil leases were agreed to yesterday. Only the formality of signing remains."

She nodded, longing to escape, longing to leave before she made an even bigger fool of herself. He had to have heard, yet he said nothing. His way of letting her down easy? "Yes. So I can go home today."

"I brought Alia with Satin Magic. I thought we could stay here for a few days. We have food, water, and the desert to ourselves."

She blinked. "Stay here? Are you nuts? There's no reason to stay here. I should be making airline reservations. My parents will be going home soon and I'll go with them. I have a job to get back to—" Not after she'd burned her bridges.

"I thought you were working with Tamil on the tourist project here. That's your job."

She pushed up on one elbow and stared at him. "What's going on?"

"I'd thought you'd stay."

"Why?"

"You love me."

She flopped back on the pillow and closed her eyes again. He had heard!

"And you have a job to do."

"I didn't tell Pete about us. He tweaked some of the stuff I told him and blew it out of proportion."

"Once I cooled down, and Jasmine yelled at me, I suspected that." There was definitely the sound of amusement in his tone.

She opened her eyes and glared at him.

"Are you laughing at me?"

He shook his head, but the laughter lurked in his eyes.

"Kharun, what's going on? Is this marriage over or not?"

"Ah, that's what I wanted to talk about. Don't you think people would find it odd to end it the day after the negotiations were concluded?"

"As compared to when?"

"I don't know, sometime later, so people won't think it was a false marriage."

"Sometime later?" she asked suspiciously.

"Yes."

"How much later?"

"I don't know." He looked at her sharply. "Fifty or sixty years."

She stared at him, her heart beginning to race. Had she heard him correctly? She cleared her throat.

"That's sort of a long time."

"I'm game if you are." He brushed his fingers through her hair, smiling that sexy smile that turned her bones to mush. "I love you, too, Sara. I fought it at first. One day I'll tell you about a woman I thought I loved before. But she doesn't belong with us today. I want you to stay with me forever, but I'll settle for fifty years with an option to renegotiate.''

"And you are so good at negotiating,'' she murmured, moving to meet him halfway with a kiss that sealed their future. "I love you, Kharun.''

"I was hoping you did." His kiss made her blood sing and her heart explode with happiness and love.

Then he ended the kiss. "Time's up. Come and see the sunrise," he said seconds later, throwing back the covers.

It was cold. She frowned and tried to pull the covers back, but he lifted her out of bed and placed her on her feet.

"Hurry."

"I'd rather stay in bed."

"We'll come back." He tossed her his shirt, the loose one from the night before. Sara slipped it on, tied it closed at the neck and pushed the sleeves up so her hands showed.

"Nothing's been decided. We have to discuss this.''

"We'll have the rest of our lives to discuss anything you wish. But right now, come and see the sunrise. Later this morning—before it gets too hot, we'll go riding.''

He pulled on his pants and waited impatiently by the door. Staring at his chest, she remembered the feel of him last night. Happiness and love blossomed inside, spilling out in her delightful grin. Kharun loved her! Miracles still happened.

"I thought you were furious with me.''

"I was. But love is stronger than anger. And once I

looked at things rationally, and remembered everything you'd ever said to me, I knew you would never have betrayed me.''

He'd had faith in her even when the evidence pointed the other way. She'd never had that before. It was amazing how wonderful it felt. For the first time in a long while, Sara didn't feel like a flake.

''Thank you.''

''For?''

''Believing in me.''

''And loving you?''

She laughed in joy. ''That, too. That most of all.'' She ran across the distance separating them and flung herself into his arms. ''I love you so much. I didn't want to leave, but thought it best if I left before you kicked me out.''

''Revisionist history? I believe you stormed out, I certainly didn't kick you out.''

''Well, I thought you would have, after seeing that damaging report.''

''It would never have happened. I knew long ago you were the one I wanted. I told you, one cannot fight destiny. I wasn't sure you felt the same way—especially after our arranged marriage.''

''What are you talking about? You thought I was a spy!''

He laughed softly. ''Never that. You didn't have the skills to be a spy.''

''I resent that!''

''With that honey hair and your flair, you could never fade into the background like a good spy needs to.''

"Well, you didn't trust me."

"At first, maybe, but neither did you trust me."

She was quiet for a moment, mulling over what he'd said, afraid to let herself believe what he'd said, that they'd stay married the rest of their lives. Could he truly mean it?

"You forced me into an arranged marriage," she said.

"I hear they can be the best kind. Ours will be the best."

"I love you," she said softly.

"I love you," he replied promptly. He kissed her briefly, then took her hand to lead her outside. "Forget your uncertainty, we will have a wonderful life together. Promise me you'll stay."

She smiled, her joy reflected in her eyes. "I promise!"

Sara stepped forward to greet the dawn, not only of a new day, but of her new life. A life of love and happiness with Kharun, her own desert raider. Her own desert sheikh.

There is more than one route to happiness.

Harlequin Romance® presents a gripping,
emotional two-part series from rising star

Caroline Anderson.

Destiny has more than one plan for Fran Williams—
it has two: rich, wealthy and energetic Josh Nicholson
and charming, sensual, single father Dr. Xavier Giraud!

**Can a woman choose her own destiny?
Could there be more than one Mr. Right?**

Follow Fran's parallel destinies in:

**January 2003
ASSIGNMENT: SINGLE FATHER (#3732)**

From

Plus *read about Fran's first fateful meetings with
Josh Nicholson and Xavier Giraud—for free.*

Look for DOUBLE DESTINY at www.eHarlequin.com.

For better, for worse...
these marriages were meant to last!

They've already said "I do," but what happens
when their promise to love, honor and cherish
is put to the test?

Emotions run high as husbands and wives discover
how precious—and fragile—their wedding vows
are...but their love will keep them together—forever!

Look out for the following in

MAYBE MARRIED by Leigh Michaels
(#3731) on-sale January

THE PRODIGAL WIFE by Susan Fox
(#3740) on-sale March

And watch out for other bestselling authors appearing
in this popular miniseries throughout 2003.

Available wherever Harlequin books are sold.

THE AUSTRALIANS

MEN WHO TURN YOUR
WHOLE WORLD UPSIDE DOWN!

Strong and silent...
Powerful and passionate...
Tough and tender...

Who can resist the rugged loners of the Outback?
As tough and untamed as the land they rule, they
burn as hot as the Australian sun once they meet
the women they've been waiting for.

THE WEDDING CHALLENGE
by
Harlequin Romance® rising star

Jessica Hart

on-sale February (#3736)

Feel the Outback heat throughout 2003,
with Harlequin Romance® authors:
Margaret Way, Barbara Hannay and Darcy Maguire!

*And don't miss these stories of seduction and passion by
Australian Harlequin Presents® authors:*

THE BLIND-DATE BRIDE
Emma Darcy (#2308) on-sale March

HIS CONVENIENT PROPOSAL
Lindsay Armstrong (#2324) on-sale May

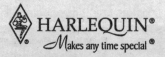

HARLEQUIN®
Makes any time special ®

If you enjoyed what you just read,
then we've got an offer you can't resist!

Take 2 bestselling
love stories FREE!
Plus get a FREE surprise gift!

Clip this page and mail it to Harlequin Reader Service®

IN U.S.A.	IN CANADA
3010 Walden Ave.	P.O. Box 609
P.O. Box 1867	Fort Erie, Ontario
Buffalo, N.Y. 14240-1867	L2A 5X3

YES! Please send me 2 free Harlequin Romance® novels and my free surprise gift. After receiving them, if I don't wish to receive anymore, I can return the shipping statement marked cancel. If I don't cancel, I will receive 6 brand-new novels every month, before they're available in stores! In the U.S.A., bill me at the bargain price of $3.34 plus 25¢ shipping & handling per book and applicable sales tax, if any*. In Canada, bill me at the bargain price of $3.80 plus 25¢ shipping & handling per book and applicable taxes**. That's the complete price and a savings of 10% off the cover prices—what a great deal! I understand that accepting the 2 free books and gift places me under no obligation ever to buy any books. I can always return a shipment and cancel at any time. Even if I never buy another book from Harlequin, the 2 free books and gift are mine to keep forever.

186 HDN DNTX
386 HDN DNTY

Name	(PLEASE PRINT)	
Address	Apt.#	
City	State/Prov.	Zip/Postal Code

* Terms and prices subject to change without notice. Sales tax applicable in N.Y.
** Canadian residents will be charged applicable provincial taxes and GST.

All orders subject to approval. Offer limited to one per household and not valid to current Harlequin Romance® subscribers.
® are registered trademarks of Harlequin Enterprises Limited.

HROM02   ©2001 Harlequin Enterprises Limited